Golgotha

a novella by

Rob Boisvert

To Mike – I hope you enjoy!

Rob

Mint Hill Books
Main Street Rag Publishing Company
Charlotte, North Carolina

Author photo on back cover by Angus Lamond Photograpy

Library of Congress Control Number: 2010920571

ISBN: 978-1-59948-233-0

Produced in the United States of America

Mint Hill Books
Main Street Rag Publishing Company
PO Box 690100
Charlotte, NC 28227-7001
www.MainStreetRag.com

To my mother, Kathleen Brown

PART ONE

Hoyle wondered if he should be worried. He stood in the kitchen in the weak morning light seeping through the windows of the farmhouse inherited from his father and into which he moved many years ago after his divorce listening again to the message on his cell phone. The room smelled of coffee and fried bacon and the dryer sheet spinning around with a load of his clothes in the dryer in the mud room. A breeze from off the mountains ballooned the yellowed curtains above the sink. As he gazed at his old, orange cat crouched on the scuffed, wooden table and nibbling at a plate of half-eaten food, he was trying to figure out what the message meant, and whether he should do anything about it.

He'd noticed the message while eating breakfast, having picked up his phone next to his keys on the table to check the time and been surprised to see the two icons for a missed call and a message. The call was from his twenty-one-year-old daughter, Christine, and came in at 1:06 A.M. It contained only one word, "Daddy," followed by thirty seconds or so of background noise in which he thought he heard passing cars and people shouting before going dead. He didn't recognize the number, and got no answer when he tried calling it. Was her voice plaintive? Exhausted? Scared? Did she sound as if she was high? Drunk? Or maybe he was overreacting. Maybe it was no big deal and she was just calling because she needed money or a place to stay. He couldn't decide. Listening to the message a third time, then grabbing his keys, he thought about phoning his ex-wife, thinking she might be able to shed some light on the reason for the call, but decided against it, considering how she felt about him.

Outside, where the air smelled like mud and something stringent like a broken sapling, he carried a bucket filled with grain from the small, timber frame barn about twenty yards from his house and inside a paddock in the ten-acre field rimmed by trees below the three mountains dubbed "The Skulls" by his father to three other buckets toppled in the dirt. The fence around the paddock was worn of paint, but sturdy and leaned outward only slightly as it disappeared into the woods. Already, the two bay geldings and one gray gelding were circling around him, snorting and making noises that sounded like raspy chuckles, the bays jostling him, and stabbing their heads into the buckets even before he finished pouring their grain. He waited a few moments until the bays were settled, then fed the gray about ten yards away from them, but as usual they abandoned their own feed and ran at the gray, heads down and necks stretched forward, driving it away, and ignoring him when he said, "Now you two get away from there. That ain't yours."

Hoyle remembered his father and how he interacted with the few horses he kept, and how the animals seemed to obey his every command. "They ain't the brightest of beasts," he heard his father say, "and it may take a while, but eventually they figure out right from wrong. Just keep at them."

Hoyle took hold of the gray by its halter and led it into the barn where it smelled of warm wood and dust and

Robert Boisvert

old, brown hay and poured a scoop of grain into another bucket, saying, "It's okay, boy. Some day they'll learn some manners," and petted the gray on the shoulder.

"Eat up quick, now," he added before leaving and securing the gate and climbing into his pickup which he'd loaded for work the previous night.

Hoyle popped in a cassette tape of *Eat a Peach* by the Allman Brothers. Turning off the gravel drive running straight from the house about one hundred yards that bisected a much smaller field where his father once raised corn and melons, and his mother planted her kitchen garden, and onto NC 22 and accelerating toward the center of Krodel about seven miles distance, Hoyle made a mental note to call a neighbor to borrow his tractor and Bush Hog. The field lay fallow now. He'd allowed a few trees to grow in it, but preferred to keep it mostly clear, liking the feeling of not being penned in as he sat on the porch after work and drank a beer or two after dinner before heading inside and nodding off in front of the TV.

Krodel lay at the intersection of Route 251 which ran south to Asheville and north across the border into Tennessee. Driving on Main Street, and passing the Dollar General store, drug store, bank, and old movie theater someone from Raleigh once tried to convert into an art gallery and antiques emporium, Hoyle parked his truck in front of and entered the Deluxe Diner, a sandwich shop owned and operated by Mary Koontz, an elderly widow who local kids called Hairy Mary because of the downy hairs that grew from her chin. The shop was empty except for Dan Sheradin, a mechanic who sat at the counter reading a newspaper and talking to Mary.

"That's why they're going to win," Hoyle heard him say as he poured himself a large coffee in a to-go cup and mixed in half-and-half and lots of sugar.

"I mean, you read about it all the time," Dan said, pointing a finger to the paper. "The Chinese don't care who they kill. A hundred people in a mine accident. A hundred more in a chemical spill. A couple thousand because of tainted milk. And that's only the stuff they report. Imagine what the real number is."

Hoyle stepped up to the counter to pay for his coffee. While pulling out his wallet, and extracting two dollar bills, he noticed Mary wasn't wearing any shoes this morning, and that her white tube socks were filthy, as if she'd been walking in mud.

"Oh, go to hell, Dan Sheradin. That's an awful thing to say," she said.

Dan grinned and slapped his hand against the countertop. "Ha! Because you know it's true. That's why."

"No, I mean it. That's awful," she said.

Dan swiveled his stool and turned to Hoyle. "You tell me if I'm wrong, Hoyle."

"I mean it," Mary said. "I don't want to hear any more of that talk."

"Let me just ask him," Dan said, still grinning. "So Hoyle, I say America and China are eventually going to go to war, and that the Chinese will win. And that's because they're the way we were a hundred years ago. Ruthless and determined. They'll do anything to make their country stronger and more advanced. Kill as many people as it takes."

Hoyle nodded his head, as if he were following Dan's train of thought, but was really trying to figure out why Mary wasn't wearing any shoes.

"While we here in the U.S.," Dan continued, "it's like we're doing everything we can to make our country weaker. You can't do this and you can't do that. Safety regulations upon safety regulations. Warning labels on everything. Like in my shop, a couple of months ago we had to stop using this lubricant I've been using for years because someone decided it causes cancer or something. So now it takes me twice as long to do something as simple as take off a rusted bolt. These guys, they make it so people can't afford to do business anymore."

"Do you even hear yourself?" Mary asked.

"We act as if death is optional," Dan said, "as if we can decide against it by avoiding any risk."

"Boy, I'm telling you, you better get your mind straight."

"Don't you see? What I'm saying is hardship makes people stronger. It makes them immune to the little wounds in life and more determined to achieve something great."

"Little wounds? Something great," Mary scoffed. "My daddy worked in a furniture plant for forty years, and the only time he missed work, he was docked a day's wages because he had to go to the hospital after cutting off the tip of his thumb building their stinking chairs and tables. What you need to do is cut out this craziness and start thinking about what's right."

"I'm just saying we've got to think about the long term."

"I mean it," Mary said.

"Hoyle, tell me I'm wrong. Tell me we aren't turning into a nation of pansies."

"Oh, get the hell out of here," Mary said. "You talk about death and misery like they were entries in a ledger book. Like none of those widows and orphans in China are missing their husbands or daddies, or shed a single tear." She grabbed and tossed his coffee cup into a bin beneath the counter. "I mean it. Get the hell out of here."

Dan was shaking his head, but still grinning as he looked at Hoyle. "Can you believe the way she talks to me?"

"Go on," Mary said. "And don't bother paying. I don't want your damned money. Just get."

Dan took his time folding his newspaper, reminding Hoyle of how the wise alecks in high school acted when they were sent to the principal's office. "See you tomorrow, Mary," he shouted without turning as he exited the door.

Mary was already wiping the counter. "Stupid bastard," she muttered.

Hoyle watched her, not sure what to say. He had never seen Mary so agitated.

"I'm sorry, Hoyle," she said, shaking her head and looking down at the floor. "It's just that that man makes me so furious with that sort of talk."

Hoyle nodded his head, noticing now her grimy hands and dirty fingernails and the matted, tangled hairs on the back of her head, as if she'd only bothered to brush the front and sides.

"I know you know what I mean," she said, gazing up at him. "I've seen it in you all your life, even when you was little." She paused a moment, as if considering her statement, then pointed her chin toward the door. "Not like that bastard. He reminds me exactly of my husband, may he rot in hell." She pursed her lips as if preparing to spit. "They act as if pain and hope ain't nothing but figments of their imagination."

Hoyle remembered the cardboard sign that had been placed in the window of the shop soon after her husband died. "Closed for death," it read. He then pictured her sitting alone in her house, spending her nights reading magazines and romance novels and—the image suddenly came to him—talking to dead friends. Her appearance worried him, and he wanted to ask if everything was alright, but hesitated, not wanting to embarrass her. Instead, he extended the two dollars for his coffee.

She took his money. "They ain't fit to tie your boot laces."

Hoyle stared at her.

Mary smiled, showing brown teeth, and hit a button on the register. "You're a good man, Hoyle Templeton. Just remember that."

Hoyle also smiled, but felt uncomfortable under her scrutiny and left the shop and climbed into his truck, having

Robert Boisvert

decided her words and strange appearance were due to the fact she worked long hours, and nothing else.

He drove faster than usual toward Asheville, not wanting to be late for the first day on this new job. The woman from Charlotte named Diane who recently moved to the area and hired him to repair the wood paneling in a library in her house struck him as strange in a way he couldn't figure. She seemed pleasant, and was attractive in the way all wealthy people are, stylish and well coifed. Maybe a little heavy in the hips and nearer his age than he at first thought. But she seemed as well rotten in some way, as if something were decaying beneath the veneer of her expensive clothes and makeup, something messy and odorous and wet, like clothes left too long in a washing machine, leaving him unsure each time he met her about how she might react to anything he said or did, or as if he were being judged in one of those TV reality shows. He would not have been surprised to discover she drank.

He arrived at her house a few minutes past 8:30. Built in the early 1900s, and surrounded by fir trees, magnolias, tulip trees and azaleas, the large house looked as if it had been cultivated from the rock of the hills, as if its slate roof and stone façade and lead windows had popped from the ground from a seed. Hoyle parked in the rear on the gravel drive beside the woman's Mercedes on top of which were set a rolled up yoga mat and water bottle.

The woman opened the door soon after he stepped out of his truck. She was smiling, and said, "You're only four minutes late." She looked up at the sky. "It's a beautiful day, isn't it? It's a shame you have to work."

Hoyle was now holding the tool box he'd hefted from the bed of his truck. "Yes, ma'am." He nodded toward the yoga mat and water bottle. "I'm sorry if I kept you from something."

"Oh, no, no, no," she said, without glancing at them. She seemed a little worried or hurt. "They're from last night.

No, no. I'm not going anywhere." She turned. "Come on in. I made some coffee."

The kitchen was spacious and smelled of coffee and cinnamon. The walls were half covered in an ivory colored subway tile which seemed as soft as icing in the morning light. In the center of the room, set amid an island of white wood topped by green granite, sat a large stainless steel gas stove that seemed as if it belonged in a restaurant. Hoyle could also smell something powdery and flowery and what might have been perfume or air freshener.

The woman moved to the counter on the other side of the island beside a refrigerator on which were several photos of a teenage boy. She wore tight fitting jeans, polished paddock boots, and a lavender colored blouse that revealed a tanned and freckled cleavage. Everything about her appearance seemed darker and more pronounced than when they'd last met: hair, eyes, lips, chin. It was as if some great hand had outlined and highlighted her features with a felt tipped pen. Hoyle felt uncomfortable watching her move—again, he couldn't figure why—as if he had stumbled upon her in a private moment.

"Can I fix you a cup of coffee?" the woman asked. She was holding a pot and ready to pour some into a mug.

"Thank you, ma'am, no," Hoyle said, holding up a hand. He wanted most to begin work.

"Please, call me Diane. You sound like one of my son's friends."

"Okay. Sorry."

Her smile broadened. "You sure?" she asked, lifting the pot higher. "Freshly brewed. I also have some cinnamon rolls straight out of the oven."

It did not surprise Hoyle to be offered something to eat and drink. The rich were like that, as if ashamed of their wealth and trying to make amends. He felt sorriest for the men who would offer him a beer in the middle of the day, as if they were foreign conquerors unsure of the local customs and trying to appease a potentially hostile native.

"That's kind. Thank you. But I ate at home."

The woman now seemed angry. Turning her back on him, and replacing the pot, she said, "Well, you know where the library is."

Hoyle stared at her back, feeling sorry for having refused her offer of food, and stepped sideways from the room, as if afraid to turn his back on her.

The library contained floor to ceiling bookshelves constructed of oak, some of which had been badly repaired years ago after a tree fell and landed on the house, damaging one wall. Whoever had completed the work botched the job by repairing the splintered and broken areas with a wood filler, which was now cracked and falling off, and by using maple in place of oak where the damage was too great to fill. Earlier, Hoyle recommended removing the damaged areas and rebuilding from scratch, saying he would be able to match the stain and finish, giving the new wood an aged patina to match the older wood.

It was work he enjoyed, and was good at, having learned it from his father. Nowadays, there wasn't much call for fine carpentry, even when hired to build kitchen and bathroom cabinets. Mostly, the jobs required little more than fitting together prefabricated sections constructed of pressed wood or plastic. When a job like this came along, which wasn't very often, he looked forward to molding and shaping the wood, and relished the warmth of it on his palms and fingertips and the sharp scent that caught on the end of his nasal passages that seemed to burst like a decayed seed.

By noon, he had removed half of what needed removing, careful not to damage the molding which he would refinish and reuse. He had not seen or heard from the woman, but he could not shake the feeling that she was hovering and he was being spied on, and he stopped and turned toward the entrance several times, listening for any telltale sign of her presence, footsteps or a creaking floorboard or even breathing. He never heard anything and wondered now as he moved toward his truck to retrieve his lunch, which he decided to eat outside, if she were even home.

He found her in the kitchen laying out four pieces of bread onto two plates.

"Oh," she said, surprised, "I was just about to ask you whether you'd prefer roast beef or ham."

Hoyle looked at the two plates. "Thank you, but I brought my lunch."

Hoyle didn't savor the idea of being forced to endure a polite lunch and conversation meant to relay the goodwill of someone who never would and did not want to be a friend. He accepted and was comfortable with his role of an employee. But seeing now the reappearance of that odd look in her eyes as if she were afraid of being hurt, or hurt again, he relented, and said, "But, ah, why don't you make yourself something and join me outside. I was thinking of eating somewhere on the grass, if that's okay."

The woman smiled and said that sounded lovely.

Outside, Hoyle retrieved a small, insulated cooler from the cab of his truck. Normally, he would have propped has back against any shade tree, but now looked around for someplace suitable for a lady to sit, wondering if he should have just accepted her invitation to eat in the kitchen, rather than forcing her to eat outside. He selected a grassy area underneath a large beech tree near a small, ornate cement bench, thinking the woman might like to sit on it, and waited. He opened the cooler, but didn't take out any of the food, feeling a little self-conscious about his selection of two peanut butter and jelly sandwiches, a half-eaten bag of Doritos, a banana, a Baby Ruth candy bar, and two cans of Coke.

The woman appeared a few minutes later, carrying a sandwich on a plate and a glass of iced tea, walking as if she were competing in one of those races in which people balance eggs on spoons. She also carried, tucked under an arm, a blue and white checkered tablecloth and matching napkins. Bending awkwardly, moving only her knees and not her back, she set the plate and glass on the bench and set to unfolding and spreading the tablecloth, telling Hoyle to smooth it on one side.

"There, that's lovely," she said, her hands on her hips. "Just like a picnic." Retrieving her food and drink, she sat with her legs to one side and nearly tucked beneath her and leaned on one arm. Hoyle sat on as little of the cloth as possible without seeming rude, not wanting to dirty it with his boots which may or may not have stepped in horse manure that morning, and emptied his cooler, all the while gazing at her sandwich, which looked like something out of an advertisement, with its fluffy, whole grain bread, dark green lettuce, and sliced meat piled high.

"It's a beautiful day," Diane said, picking up one half of the sandwich and holding it in front of her mouth, as if she were preparing to play the harmonica. "Not too hot."

Hoyle agreed. "It sure is," he said, unwrapping the tin foil surrounding his two sandwiches which he would fold and reuse. At any other time, he would have told her to help herself to his chips, but for some reason wondered if she would be insulted by the offer. After taking a large bite out of a sandwich, and swallowing quickly, he said, "You have a nice yard."

Diane looked around as if she were surveying the area for the first time, her eyes settling for seconds at a time on various groups of flowers and plantings. "A lot of it was here when I bought the place, but I started sprucing things up and changing them in the Spring. I've always liked to garden. I like watching things grow." She nibbled at her sandwich. "What about you? Do you like it?"

Hoyle struggled to swallow, dislodging mashed peanut butter and bread from the roof of his mouth. "No, not really. My father planted corn and melons and sometimes alfalfa when I was growing up. So I guess I always equated gardening with work."

The woman smiled, then tweezed a seed from the crust of her bread with two red fingernails. There then followed a couple of minutes of silence in which Hoyle chewed hurriedly and washed each mouthful down with Coke, preparing to answer any number of personal questions about his youth and family and work and what sorts of things he liked to do. He remembered one guy who'd hired him once asking if women minded the feel of his calloused hands, and whether the calluses made it more difficult to appreciate touching a breast. But the woman surprised him by saying, "You don't really want to be here, do you?"

She held up a hand, as if to forestall any objection. "I'm sorry. It was stupid, my forcing you to have lunch like this. I should have just left you alone." She was smiling, but Hoyle assumed she was about to cry, the way she held one hand over her mouth.

He didn't know what to do. He was holding a sandwich, and felt stupid and almost heartless holding it, but didn't want to move for fear of drawing attention to himself or insulting her by acting seemingly selfishly by either putting it down or taking a bite from it.

"I do this all the time," she continued. "I feel a little bit of a connection with someone and I get all excited and go overboard and try to force things, try to cram things into place where maybe they don't belong.

"You know the thing they never tell you about divorce?" she asked. "All those self-help books and counselors and divorce attorneys? It's what to do with all those unplugged wires that at one time were connected to another person. They talk about intimacy and say every person deserves to be intimate with someone else, equating it with romance and love. But they don't tell you that intimacy isn't good or bad, that there isn't a good form of it or bad form. That instead it's a state of being, and that it can satisfy a portion of a person even without love, or even with hatred. I mean, I hated my husband the last few years of our marriage—hated him—and knew he didn't give a damn about me for most of the twenty-one years we were together. But one word from him, a grunt as he stumbled toward the bathroom in the morning would satisfy me and hit me in more ways and seem more meaningful than hours of conversation with friends and anything I've endured since we split. Sometimes, I feel as if I'm walking around trying to communicate to a world of dogs, that everyone around me understands one or two words of what I'm saying, but misses everything else. Do you know what I mean?"

The way Diane looked at him, the way her blue eyes seemed to glint like a knife and hone in on his wherever he moved them suggested he needed to take care. He knew if he said the wrong thing, if he offered a platitude or lied she would never again speak to him, at least not in this manner. A part of him wondered if maybe that would be a good thing, that it would ensure that their relationship remained on a purely professional level. But he worried about her overreacting and feeling shunned and firing him from a job he'd looked forward to performing. Plus, and despite being embarrassed by her naked honesty, he felt sorry for her to a degree that surprised him and seemed almost inordinate, surprised by the tenderness he felt for what she offered, as if her honesty were a baby in need of nourishment and comfort. He stared at her hands that seemed as soft as taffy in a small patch of sunlight on the blue and white cloth, afraid to look into her eyes.

"I don't know," he said. "What you're saying makes sense, but I never felt it." He shrugged his shoulders, hoping the small gesture would convey his sincerity and desire to empathize with her. "My ex-wife and I were only married for three years, and that was nineteen years ago. And while we were married, I always felt like the odd man out. I remember thinking it was as if I was her second best husband, as if I was an afterthought. It was like she was having these deep conversations with someone, like she would go in the bedroom and close the door and in there would have the sort of conversation she was supposed to have with her husband, as if she was speaking to a ghost, or a sort of make believe friend of her ideal mate, and then afterwards come out and talk to me about nothing. About what we should have for dinner, or complain about our baby daughter or her job or lack of money and what she wanted to buy and couldn't afford. That intimacy you're talking about, we never had it. I wanted it, but for three years I felt like a pinball in constant motion, always bouncing off of her." He was relieved to see her smiling when he finally did look up at her.

"So what does a person do?" she asked.

Hoyle again shrugged his shoulders. "I don't know. Become friends with yourself, I guess. I don't know much about you, but you seem like a decent person, someone worth knowing. I guess start there."

The way Diane now gazed at him redoubled his embarrassment and caused him to grow uneasy, as if she were conveying a secret he wasn't sure he wanted to learn.

He thought about her and how she looked at him for the remainder of the day after they finished their lunch and discussed movies and television shows and he returned to work in the library. None of it made any sense. He guessed she was attracted to him, or at least she seemed to be toying with the idea, but he did not see himself as the type of person she would ever date. And he could not decide if he was attracted to her. He liked looking at her, but she continued to strike him as odd, sort of like those few misfit teenagers he remembered from high school, alternately and naively pessimistic and optimistic and making a big show of both. It had been a year since he'd dated anyone. Barbara who worked at the Red Rock Tavern, a bar where he sometimes shot pool. They remained friendly. And, anyway, he knew he would never ask her out. He supposed it was because he did not want to endure seeing his life through her eyes, watching this well-to-do woman survey and assess his old house with furniture inherited from his parents, his rundown truck, his few friends, his lack of hobbies, his cheap clothes.

He tried to forget about Diane and stop thinking about what should and shouldn't happen and concentrate fully on the work. Once, when a strip of molding he was prying off cracked and splintered, he grew so annoyed with himself he nearly cursed out loud. But, again, he couldn't shake the feeling he was being watched, and that Diane was listening somewhere close by, and was relieved to leave the house at four o'clock, after hauling the refuse from the shelves outside and stacking it neatly by the driveway, feeling as if he had loosened his belt after a fattening meal, telling her in the kitchen that he had finished all he could that day without purchasing lumber and that he would return the next day with what he needed.

Diane stood with her arms crossed and backside leaned against the countertop. She was holding a glass of wine. "Maybe we can have lunch again outside, if the weather is nice," she said, her voice conveying both hope and fear.

"Yes," Hoyle lied, "that would be nice."

Hoyle then drove to a lumber yard on the outskirts of Asheville that smelled of cut and burned timber where he first chatted with the elderly owner who'd been friends with his father before walking to the section of the warehouse containing the best and seasoned selection of wood. He made a list of what he needed and took his time picking the boards, running his hands along the length of them and checking their grain to be sure each was as close to center cut as possible to avoid any warping. He knew he was dallying, maybe taking more time than was really necessary, but he felt comforted by the process, as if he were relaxing in a steam room and could feel his anxiety oozing off his body and beading on his skin like sweat.

When his cell phone rang, just as he loaded the last of the boards onto a cart, he at first feared it might be Diane calling, inviting him to dinner. He looked at the number and was surprised and worried to see it belonged to Karen, his ex-wife. Karen lived in Asheville where she worked as a waitress at the Grove Park Inn, a resort and spa built in the Nineteenth Century.

"Hello," he said, bracing himself for bad news. Karen and he hadn't spoken in nearly two years. The last time he'd seen her more than a year ago at a grocery store she pretended not to notice him and ignored his wave.

"I've kicked Christine out of the house," Karen said, "and wanted to make sure you don't give her any money."

Hoyle stood still in the aisle, one hand gripping the cart. "Why? What happened?"

"What do you think happened? Jesus. She's using again. I warned her. One more time and she's out."

"Is she okay? Do you know where she is?"

"Are you not hearing what I'm saying? I told you, I kicked her out of the house. How should I know where she is?"

Karen's tone of voice full of exasperation and disgust flooded him with memories of when they fought during their few years of marriage and caused him to feel just as it did then, inadequate and hollow, each of her words piercing through him as if through a Japanese lantern. He knew if he objected to it she would grow furious and refuse to speak about anything else. He decided not to tell her Christine called sometime the previous night.

"I know. I heard you," he said. "I'm just wondering if you have any idea where she went."

"Who knows? Probably shacking up with that loser boyfriend of hers."

"What's his name?"

"Hoyle, what the fuck does that matter? Just don't give her any goddamned money, okay? Let her see what life is like without someone else paying the bills."

Robert Boisvert

Hoyle wasn't surprised when she hung up on him, and pushed the phone into a pocket and leaned his weight onto the cart, heading toward the checkout counter, as if all his calls ended in the same manner.

But he was worried now, certain that his ex-wife could only have stomached calling him if the trouble between her and Christine were much worse than normal. After paying for the wood and loading it onto the bed of his truck, he sat for a few minutes in the cab, wondering what he should do. He considered phoning Karen and trying to wheedle from her more information about Christine's latest boyfriend, maybe finding out where he lived. Instead, though, he started the truck, having decided to head back to Asheville to see if he could find her. On the way, he redialed the number Christine had called him from the previous night, getting no response.

The streets were more crowded than he would have expected for a Monday with tourists and locals and those artists and vagrants dressed in dirty jeans and tie dye T-shirts who loitered on the sidewalks performing magic tricks or music for small change. He didn't like Asheville and rarely spent time in its many bars and restaurants and art galleries, feeling always depressed and dirty and infected afterwards, as if he were returning from a visit to a leper colony, or some horrible version of the Land of Misfit Toys in the *Rudolph the Red Nosed Reindeer* Christmas special he'd first seen on television as a child.

Driving slowly along North Lexington Avenue and Broadway and College Street and around Pritchard Park and Pack Square, trying to spot Christine or any friends he remembered from the last time he'd seen her, he felt worse than usual, seeing how people began eventually to stare at him, especially the older vagrants, drunken grizzled men, some without shirts or with bandanas tied around their heads who seemed angered by his appearance, as if worried his unseemly designs might hinder their own. He felt conspicuous and foolish and wished he could proceed on foot, but didn't want to risk parking his truck and having someone steal his tools or load of wood. He gave up shortly after stopping at a stop light and asking a group of three people, one young man and two women, if they knew his daughter and where he might find her. The man, a tall and skinny white guy with dreadlocks and a beard and wearing a T-shirt that hung almost to his knees, said nothing and answered by extending an arm and pointing to the horizon and spinning around in circles. Both women sniggered.

Hoyle drove away and toward home feeling unaccomplished and a failure in more ways than he could identify. Remembering Christine as a toddler and how beautiful she looked in the dresses his mother sewed, he ached to hold and comfort her and to feel and marvel again at her pudgy legs and arms and the firmness of her skin. Nearing Krodel, and at a corner gas station and country store known locally for its grilled liver mush sandwiches, he was relieved to see Lt. Travis Clydefelter standing beside a cruiser, filling it with fuel.

"I'm glad to see you're still finding work, or at least I'm hoping you are," Travis said, glancing at the wood in Hoyle's truck after Hoyle veered in next to him. Travis joined the sheriff's office after a stint in the Marine Corps during which he served in the Gulf War, once telling Hoyle it was no more glorious than standing guard in a latrine. The two played baseball together in high school and remained friendly. "The way you sped in like that you reminded me of my sons wanting to borrow money."

Hoyle smiled, but could think of nothing clever to say. He exited the truck.

"You okay?" Travis asked.

"I was wondering if you've seen Christine anywhere."

Travis ignored the gas pump when it clicked off once the cruiser's tank was filled. "She using again?"

"I guess so. Karen called today. Said she kicked her out. Said she was probably staying with some boyfriend of hers.

"Karen called, eh?" Travis knew about the history between Hoyle and his ex. "Yeah, I've seen her once or twice with this kid Shawn Shiflette. A real piece of work."

"Do you know where he lives?"

"He used to have a place over by the Red Roof Inn in Asheville. I don't know if he still does. But I tell you what. Why don't you let me check it out? He's a mean bastard, and smart. We know he's cooking meth, but have never been able to find out where. And you should see his family. Christ. They're like a pack of wild dogs, fighting over meat. You remember when Mike Tyson bit off a part of Evander Hollyfield's ear? I once arrested Shawn's mother for doing the same thing to one of her daughters-in-law." Travis removed the nozzle from the gas tank and replaced it on the pump. "I'll ask around tomorrow, see what I can find out, and give you a call."

"Thanks. I appreciate that," Hoyle said.

Travis opened the door of the cruiser. "Really. You okay?"

Hoyle shifted his weight and shrugged his shoulders. "You know."

Travis said: "I hear you. But don't worry." He climbed into the car. "Christine might like to get high. But she isn't stupid. She'll keep herself out of too much trouble. I'll give you a call."

Hoyle felt better, watching the man drive away, knowing he would keep his word. At the same time, however, he felt a twinge of resentment spurred by the suspicion that maybe Travis knew and understood his daughter better than he did, and might be of more help to her. Driving home, and feeling guilty about the resentment and all at once worn out, as if his blood were draining from his body like oil from an oil pan, he tried to remember the last time he'd spoken to Christine, whether it had been on Christmas or not, and the time before that. Now at his house, and after backing his truck through the gate in the paddock fence and into the barn to keep the wood dry just in case it rained, though he doubted it would considering the clearness of the darkening sky and crisp smell of the gloaming like a sliced apple, he fed the horses, then his cat, and spent the remainder of the evening watching a movie on HBO and trying not to worry about what she was doing at any given moment, whether she was laughing with friends or crying alone, or where she would sleep.

He awoke earlier than normal the next morning, feeling energized and anxious and wishing he could throw on his clothes and drive right away to Diane's and begin work. He killed time instead by cooking breakfast and finishing his daily chores, including currying and brushing the gray gelding and pulling briars from its tail, which the gelding seemed to like by the way it leaned into him and lowered its head and groaned as it breathed. After packing his lunch and loading his tools, and when finally he could climb into his truck, he felt relieved driving to Asheville, liking the feel of the cool air huffing through an open window on his face and chest, and how it seemed to pin his anxiety into place.

Backing his truck to the rear entrance of Diane's house, and jumping out, he dodged the woman's offer of coffee and muffins by lying and saying he needed to carry the wood into the house as soon as possible so as to avoid exposing it to excess humidity, which seemed to work by the way she raised her eyebrows and frowned, as if to say, "I didn't know that." Hoyle worked fast, laying out a tarp to protect the floor and stacking the wood, all the while trying to ignore Diane standing in the kitchen who, each time he entered or exited the house, made some sort of comment, such as, "Oof, that looks heavy," or "Let me know if I can help," or "You're like a machine, the way you work."

He was sweating and breathing heavily by the time he finished and began unreeling a drop chord on the driveway and setting up his work horses and table and miter saws, but at last felt more relaxed and able to tolerate Diane and not feel the need to shun or run away from her when she again offered him a cup of coffee. They stood in the kitchen, each of them on different sides of the island.

"Do you own horses?" she asked.

The question surprised him, until he remembered grooming the gray gelding. "Sorry. Do I stink?"

"No, I love the smell. I used to take lessons and miss riding. How many do you own?"

"Three. But they're not much to look at. I don't exercise them near as much as I should."

"Do you ride near where you live?"

Hoyle nodded his head. "Back behind my property. There's an old logging road leading up into the mountains."

"Oh, I bet that must be pretty. Especially this time of year," she said. "We should go riding sometime."

The way she said the last line, quick and breathy, Hoyle could tell she'd been aiming for it all the while, and was relieved when she turned away to empty and rinse her cup in the sink, as if her courage had fled, allowing him to recover from his surprise. He was smiling by the time she turned back around, and said, "Yeah, that would be nice."

He agreed to eat lunch again with Diane and felt better when he began to work, thinking he'd been wrong about her and that she wasn't as odd as he at first thought, just friendly and open and wanting someone to converse with who didn't offer only platitudes. He thought about her smile and how attractive it was and how her eyes seemed to pop and fizzle like fireworks as he glued and clamped together two eight-by-two boards to be used as upright supports on the shelves, which he would later cut to measure and plane. Grabbing the old trim which he'd removed the previous day, and carrying it outside to the far edge of the driveway near an old pump house painted green, he began applying varnish remover, slathering it onto the wood with a paint brush, which he would leave for several hours until the finish started to loosen and bubble, and thinking at the same time it wouldn't be all that bad eating lunch with the woman and learning more about her life and what brought her to the mountains.

Hoyle was back inside working, scraping old varnish and dirt from the floor and prepping it for new construction when he received a call from Travis.

"It's not great news," the man said. "I rode over to that guy I was telling you about, Shawn, his last known address. Seems he's not living there anymore, and I'm not sure where he's living now. But I checked with a buddy of mine on the Asheville PD and described Christine to him. Pretty girl, long brunette hair, taller than most, a little plump. He says he thinks he's seen the two of them hanging out together in the downtown area. Thinks she might even be selling, though he couldn't be sure. And he didn't see her name on any arrest records."

Hoyle thought any collection of words would seem inadequate and trite in light of how he felt. He thanked his friend, feeling powerless, as if he were standing on the edge of a great white space of clouds with no horizon that seemed about to envelop and absorb him, like sugar in water. Going back to work, and trying to concentrate only on whatever inch of floor he was scraping, he did not think again about Diane until she retrieved him for lunch.

"What's wrong?" she asked after they were settled on the same patch of grass as the previous day. "You haven't said a half dozen words since we've been out here."

Hoyle shook his head and tried to smile. "It's nothing."

"Is it me? Am I coming on again too strong again? I didn't mean anything by the invitation to ride," she said. "It was really more of a joke than anything." She was staring at the remainder of her sandwich and tapping it with a forefinger, as if trying to awaken and shoo it away. "You don't have to stay here. I won't be offended and won't do anything crazy like fire you."

Hoyle was again surprised by the sudden strength of the sympathy he felt for her. "It's nothing like that," he said, pushing aside that portion of himself and an accompanying fear that told him to keep quiet, sensing he would somehow be indebted to her for listening to him. He shook his head again, not knowing where to begin or how much to divulge. "It's just that I got a call from a friend of mine with the sheriff's office. See, my daughter, Christine, has been hooked on methamphetamine off and on for a number of years. She's a sweet kid, but my ex-wife kicked her out of the house a couple of days ago. And my friend just told me she's hanging around with this dangerous character and maybe dealing drugs."

"How old is she?" Diane was staring at him in a way that caused him to blush and to think for a moment she might kiss him, as ridiculous as that seemed, the way she breathed through her opened mouth and extended her lower lip.

"Twenty-one," he said.

"I know you want to protect her," she said. "It's only natural. But she's a grown woman. She's not a child anymore. You can't protect her from every bump and bruise that comes her way. My son is nineteen. He's in college and, thankfully, hasn't gotten into too much trouble in life. He's made some stupid mistakes, like everybody. And I'm sure he'll make some more. But I know there's nothing I can do about that, and that I just have to accept it, and try my best to be there when and if he needs me and seeks me out."

Hoyle had raised his eyebrows and was nodding his head. "I know you're right. But I can't help feeling that I need to do more, that she needs me." He was thinking about the message his daughter left on his cell phone.

"Every parent feels that way. I still feel that way with my son. And I'm sure my parents still feel that way about me. My God, you should hear my mother when she calls, asking if I'm eating enough and telling me I should take vitamins."

"I know. But maybe I should have done more. Maybe I should have helped her more, steered her away from this sort of life."

"Were you there when she needed you? Did you give her the things she needed?"

"She was raised mostly by my ex-wife."

"But what about you? Did you give her the things she needed? I mean, it's obvious you love her."

Hoyle didn't know the answer to her questions and, because he didn't, felt a great sense of guilt. "I tried to. I wanted to."

"Hoyle, look at me," she said. "You've done all you could as a parent. I'm certain of that just by the amount of affection and anxiety I hear in your voice. No one can predict how the world will touch any of us, or what the future holds. You can do everything perfectly, say the right things, act the right way, plan for the future, and still be disappointed, and never really know why. Something you said, didn't say, did, didn't do. You'll hear explanations, but more often than not they won't make sense, as if you're accused of crimes you didn't and couldn't ever commit by people who live in an upside down world and pray to an uncaring god. I'm telling you, you've got to accept it's not your fault for how your daughter is acting."

Hoyle suspected Diane was referring to something other than his relationship with Christine—probably, she was talking about her marriage—but was grateful nonetheless. He couldn't remember if she'd called him by his name before, and felt thrilled when she used it and closer to her, as if she'd reached across the tablecloth to hold his hand.

Even so, and despite his inner acknowledgment that she was probably right, he couldn't wrench himself free of the belief that he needed to help his daughter and reach out to her and offer her whatever assistance she desired. And so after stripping the trim and applying a second coat of varnish remover which he would allow to sit overnight, and finishing work for the day, and leaving his tools at Diane's, he drove again to Asheville, this time parking his truck and setting out on foot.

He walked for close to an hour, smelling the food in different restaurants and car exhaust and various perfumes and colognes on the people crowding the sidewalks, before seeing Christine sitting on a curb at Pack Square, talking with a girl about her own age and smoking a cigarette, her elbows on her knees. She was wearing an old skirt that seemed as if it had been stitched from a threadbare sheet, some sort of thick soled sandals, and a brown crocheted cap. On both arms and around her neck were strung a mass of bracelets and necklaces, the shininess of which only heightened the dreariness and slovenliness of her overall appearance.

Hoyle felt shock when he saw her, and approached slowly, not wanting to see and be further saddened by her greasy hair and skin and dirty fingernails and hairy legs and stains on her clothing. For a moment, just as he moved within the last ten yards and saw that she hadn't yet noticed him, he even considered turning and crossing the street, wondering if maybe she might be embarrassed by his appearance and that it might be best if he allowed her the freedom and time to find her own way home, either to her mother's or his place.

"Hello, Christine," he said. He stood in front of her with his hands in his pockets so that his shadow fell over her.

Both Christine and the other girl looked at him with the same quizzical expression.

"What are you doing here?" Christine asked. "I thought you hated Asheville."

Hoyle glanced at the other girl before looking again at his daughter. It occurred to him then that she didn't understand he was here to help her, which wasn't what he expected. Picturing finding her, as he had many times over the last two days, he imagined she would either laugh or cry, and not stare at him as if she were trying to add a column of figures in her head.

"I'm here to see if you're alright," he explained. "Your mother called me and told me she kicked you out."

Her expression now changed to one of incredulity. "Mom called you? You must have thought I was dead."

"No, no. Your mother was worried about you," he said, not wanting to reveal too much and cause her to grow defensive. "She just wanted to let me know about the situation."

"Yeah, right," she scoffed. She smiled, revealing yellow teeth. "She's probably just pissed that she'll have to find someplace else to buy her coke."

Hoyle felt a weight in the pit of his stomach, hearing what she said, and a flash of shame because of the ugliness of the comment.

"Don't say that," he said, having assumed Christine was lying and lashing out at her mother. "She means well."

Christine again expressed bafflement, and shook her head after dragging on her cigarette. She then flicked it past him onto the street. "What do you want?"

"I came to see you. After you called me the other night, I wanted to see that you were okay."

She scrunched her eyes. "I didn't call you."

Hoyle now felt embarrassed and wondered if he'd been wrong. "Yes you did. You left a message."

"When?"

"The other night. Sunday night. You left it at one in the morning. You said, 'Daddy,' and that was it."

She shook her head. "Well, if I did, I don't remember. Sorry."

His embarrassment grew. "Okay. Well, are you alright? You can stay with me. Or I've got money if you need it."

"Sure. Whatever," she said. "I'll take your money."

Hoyle stood for a moment gazing at her before reaching into a back pocket for his wallet, wondering if her indifference was feigned or real. He handed her seventy dollars, everything he had.

Christine looked at the money placed in the palm of her hand as if she were about to spit on it. "That all you got?"

Hoyle was about to say, "I can get more," when he was shoved from behind and heard, "Yo, man, what the fuck you doing?"

Hoyle turned around. The first thing he noticed about the man who pushed him were his dark brown eyes that glistened like wet lollipops and seemed to shiver or vibrate like tuning forks. The young man in his mid-twenties was shorter than Hoyle by a good four inches and skinnier, but seemed somehow dangerous and tenacious, like a feral cat. He wore his hair cut short, revealing a scar on the right side of his scalp, a green, tight-fitting T-shirt, and jeans that seemed to have been dragged through the mud.

"Don't none of you old fuckers own the Internet?" he asked. "Shit, man, I told you before you need to jerk off at home and quit bothering my women."

Hoyle felt more saddened than scared to realize his daughter wanted more of a relationship with this man than him. "You must be Shawn," he said.

The man narrowed his eyes, staring at him with suspicion. "Who the hell are you?"

"He's nobody, Shawn," Christine said. "Leave him alone." Hoyle could not tell if her tone of voice expressed exasperation or fear.

"No. Who the hell is he to be talking to me like he knows me?"

"He's my father, Shawn. He just came to see if I'm alright."

Hoyle suspected the man was now playacting at being confused.

"What do you mean alright?" Shawn asked. He was staring at Hoyle. "Why wouldn't she be alright?"

Hoyle knew it would do no good saying anything else to the man, that the man was goading and testing him. Shaking his head, his sadness deepening, he turned to Christine. "You can call me anytime. For anything."

"Aw, that's sweet," Shawn said. "Touching. A real Oprah moment."

Hoyle resisted looking again at him. "Okay?" he asked his daughter.

Christine said nothing.

"I'd invite you to tuck her in tonight," Shawn said, "but you might be embarrassed by what you see next." He'd sidled close to Hoyle and was whispering. "That girl's nasty, man. Did you know that?"

Hoyle wanted to close his eyes and be transported into his truck. He wanted to instill in his daughter's mind the reality of the situation she was in and to cause her to recognize the foulness of Shawn and to see into the future the regret she would feel for wasting so much time with him. One word. He wondered if maybe there remained one word he left unsaid that would awaken and spur that realization, and was loathe to leave for fear that he might have missed it laying about like a penny on the street, or that it would occur to him later when he was at home and eating dinner, or that she herself would find it, remembering it like the name of a long lost friend.

But Hoyle knew there was nothing left to be said, and no reason to remain, and so turned and crossed the street, hearing Shawn yelling, "Give me a call if you decide to drop over," and feeling all the while under his and Christine's gazes as if he were dissolving back to front, molecule by molecule, so that he could see drifting from over his shoulder bits of skin and flesh and bone floating on the wind like dandelion spore. He moved hurriedly, wanting to exit their horizon, and felt a fool when he needed to dodge two cars, thinking he had never felt as profound a sadness for himself and for Christine and the friend she sat beside and even Shawn, wanting to embrace his daughter so closely she might feel his heart and to give her his love he carried like a gift he hoped might calm her mind and give her happiness. Back at his truck, and after starting the engine, he sat a moment thinking of a route home that would avoid the square to hide from her.

Over the next few days, and especially at night, he never went anywhere without his phone, even taking it into the bathroom, hoping to hear from her. At night, he slept uneasily, fearing he might not hear the ringer. But Christine never called, and in time he accepted the fact that he couldn't salve her wounds—not yet, anyway—and that he couldn't preoccupy himself with whether they would bleed out and scab up or whether she might ever need or want his ministrations. It was a subject he and Diane discussed over lunch, she saying he couldn't help people who didn't know they needed help, and that such a state of mind was rare in an individual's life and arose usually only just before death.

The two of them continued to eat each day in her yard, Diane growing more relaxed and effusive over time. She told him about her marriage, and about the many affairs of her husband, the owner of a medical supply company, and how eventually he could endure having sex with her only while simultaneously watching pornographic videos on the Internet or television. Each day, her stories grew more intimate and woeful, she telling him she decided to move to the mountains after driving home one night after drinking with friends and realizing she wouldn't have cared in the least if her car swerved towards a tree.

At first, Hoyle kept quiet, and only nodded when appropriate, not knowing what to say, and feeling uncomfortable and ashamed hearing the raw details of her life, and almost as he did those few times he'd visited strip clubs years ago and wanted to turn away from the women gyrating in front of him, feeling more sorry for them than aroused. Eventually, though, after she began to cry with a certain regularity, and he saw how the tears seemed to transform her physically, causing her face to appear less pinched and stern and more pliable, and her body more languorous and almost liquid-like in its movements like mercury, he began to soften and offer his opinions, his profound sadness for her transforming into that heightened level of sorrow that produces indignity. He told her he understood her pain, and that she had been wronged by her ex-husband, and that she shouldn't feel guilty and second guess her actions and motivations; that she had been brave to move to the mountains and start fresh, and that she was an intelligent, intuitive, and attractive woman, even beautiful, who needn't worry about her future. Until eventually he began to look forward to listening to her, and enjoyed dwelling upon her situation and various problems while working or late at night at his house, wondering how he might help, so much so it did not faze him or seem out of the ordinary when she invited him for a quick meal at a nearby restaurant, and later that night cried on his shoulder while sitting in her car and kissed him, saying, "Thank you, thank you, you saved my life," the words seeming to worm their way though his head and settle in his stomach, satisfying him and feeling warm like a first sip of coffee in the morning.

They did not sleep together until three weeks later after riding on horseback into the mountains. By now, Hoyle had finished working on her library, and moved on to another job, building a deck onto a house not too far from Diane's for a man who wore a silver bracelet in the shape of a snake and a ring on one of his thumbs. They still saw each other nearly every day, and spoke by phone several times a day, she calling to tell him about something she'd seen on TV or read on the Internet, or offering tips on how to improve and expand his business. But he shied from showing her his house, thinking she might be disappointed and that the sight of it might break this pleasant spell they seemed to be under, and cause her to view him as a lesser breed of man, until she wheedled him into taking her riding, saying she felt safe with him, and that she believed it would be therapeutic for her and help her reconnect with the happier moments of her life.

Hoyle agreed and set a date for a Saturday morning, but continued to feel uneasy about it, even after spending much of the previous night scrubbing his house, and even more so when he watched her Mercedes roll down his drive that morning and saw her through the windshield smiling and waving to him on the porch, the shiny car looking as out of place on his property as a tiara in a pile of leaves.

"Oh, I love it. It's beautiful," she said, as soon as she exited the car, and insisted on seeing every room. Hoyle said little on the tour, not commenting when she said, "You know, some of this stuff might be worth a lot of money," and shuffled her outside as soon as possible, feeling relieved and less constricted and, in an odd way, more at home in the barn, gathering tack for their ride.

He decided it would be best if she rode the gray and he took the taller of the two bays. The horses hadn't been ridden much since he injured a knee on a job a couple of years ago. But at least the gray was gentle natured and wouldn't charge ahead or buck or try to avoid the bit. After tacking the horses, and mounting, and Hoyle checked to be sure Diane seemed steady in the saddle, which she did, they set out at an easy pace toward the rear of the property and the path that led into the mountains.

The path was cut by his father not long after Hoyle was born and tied into an old logging road that in spots was little more than two ruts between second growth that rose up over the hill where his property ended before winding around the first of three small mountains dubbed the Skulls because of the flat expanse of rock atop each of them that at a certain angle resembled human skulls. Stretching in a line east to west and descending in height, and despite never having been owned by his family, the mountains had always seemed to him like his own private stoop and portal to a broader range stretching into Tennessee. As a youngster and teen, he would often slip away alone to ride or walk the road between the pine and maple trees and sometimes into the woods where each time he would discover something new and always towards the rocky plateau atop the first and tallest of the Skulls and sit and gaze at the vista that seemed the end of the world, and rightly so, and feel energized and grateful by what he beheld, as if the valleys and distant mountains were a swimming pool into which he might dive.

Riding now side-by-side, the horses already laboring and breathing hard, Hoyle and Diane said little as they crossed the hill until the bay began flicking its head at every other step and attempted to nip the gray.

"What's he doing?" Diane asked. She was smiling. "Doesn't your horse like mine?"

"Horses congregate by colors," Hoyle said, his voice hesitant. He didn't want to seem like a know-it-all. "And they have a distinctive pecking order. The two bays stick together, and they gang up on the gray."

"Really? That's not very nice."

Hoyle shrugged his shoulders. "No, but it's just the way it is. What can you do?"

By the time they reached the open and flat stretch between the hill and the first Skull, the sun had broken through the morning haze and began to weigh heavily on their shoulders. Hoyle could smell the sunlight on the long yellow grass and second growth and how it amplified the smell of the horses and saddle leather and blankets.

Smiling, and looking at him mischievously, her lips and teeth glistening in the sunlight, Diane urged the gray into a canter, giggling as it ran ahead.

They slowed to a trot, and then a walk as they began ascending the first Skull where the trees formed a sort of canopy and the air grew cooler and smelled like pine sap. The bay took another moment to settle and pranced sideways and shook his head, trying to slip the bit.

"What's that?" Diane asked, pointing to an old tree stand, now half covered in vines. "One of your old forts?"

"It's a tree stand my father and I used to use." Not stopping, he gestured with a chin toward some scrub to their left. "There used to be a deer path right there. Actually, there might still be, for all I know. It's been a long time."

Diane seemed not to understand what he was saying and took a moment to respond. "You mean it's for hunting?"

"Yeah. You wait there either early in the morning or late in the afternoon when you know the deer are heading to water."

Diane turned to look at the stand now behind her, then at him. "You hunt?" Her tone suggested she expected an apology, rather than an answer.

"Not anymore."

"But you used to."

"When my father was alive."

She took another moment, and spoke now as if she regretted her earlier tone.

"What did you hunt?"

"Mostly deer and turkey. Sometimes squirrels. Sometimes rabbits." Without turning, he jerked a thumb over a shoulder. "That open area we passed just before we hit the mountain is loaded with rabbits."

"Squirrels?" She made a face as if she were disgusted.

Hoyle smiled. "They're good in stew."

"Did you like it? Hunting, I mean."

Hoyle looked up at the trees, remembering being excited as a child as he toted his .22 through the woods. He remembered the way his father crooked his own rifle under an arm and marched between the trees in his woolen and red plaid jacket, as if he were always heading home and confident about his direction.

"Don't panic," he heard him say. "You get lost, just head uphill. People always want to head downhill when they don't know where they're going. I guess maybe because it feels comforting, having gravity propel them in a certain direction, like it's some sort of divine force bolstering their instinct to flee. But don't be fooled. It might seem harder, but eventually you'll get to the top of someplace and can see where you need to go next."

Hoyle turned to Diane. "I liked being with my dad. And being outdoors in the woods," he said. "It always felt right and peaceful and never complicated, as if this was really where I belonged and everyplace else was a mistake. Like I was a fish that'd been thrown back into water and didn't have to struggle any longer to figure out how to breathe. Or at least it seemed that way with my father. We didn't say much when we were out here. But every time I came home I felt as if I'd spent the day discussing everything under the sun. It was funny because my mother would look at us and shake her head, saying we were keeping secrets from her. Not in a bad way. Just sort of ribbing us for how we'd seem all pleased with ourselves."

"So why'd you give it up? Was it because your father died?"

Hoyle nodded his head. "Mostly. Part of it was because my ex-wife didn't like it. Thought it was stupid, a waste of time. She also didn't like my father. Thought he was weak. But mostly it was because of him, because after he died the whole thing became something else, something much less satisfying. Hunting became just hunting, just a long walk to shoot a rifle and to kill something. I began to feel bad for the animals, especially if I didn't get off a clean first shot, and I'd feel sorry for them as I watched the light pass from their eyes. And I didn't like how those feelings seemed to sully my memories and what I loved most about the pastime. So I just quit. One fall, hunting season came and I decided to go to the movies instead."

The two of them rode in silence for a few minutes, Diane seeming to nibble on his words like crackers.

"How many guns do you own?" she asked, asking the question as if she were a child and excited by the danger of handling a weapon.

"Four. Two rifles, a shotgun, and a pistol."

"Really?"

Hoyle was a little disappointed that she didn't comment on his explanation, wanting her to embrace his past, and feeling now as if it were just another reminder of how different they were, but smiled, thinking how funny it was that city people always reacted to talk about guns in the same way, and wondered if someday they'd express the same amazement when someone admitted owning a hammer or saw or any other tool.

Forty minutes later they emerged from beneath the canopy and into the open at the top of the mountain. The rocky plateau lay like the top two tiers of a wedding cake, rising up steeply before leveling off, then rising again onto a single, flat expanse of granite about one hundred square yards worn smooth by eons of snow and rain. Hoyle dismounted on the rise before the first tier where he tied the horses to two scrub pines a short distance from each other where they might graze on the small amount of grass growing in the open between jutting rocks. Taking Diane by the hand, who was looking around as he hoped she might, he led her up the first tier, then the second, telling her to be careful on the slippery rock. At the top, where the sunlight reflecting off the granite caused them to squint and a soft breeze carried the scents of pine and dirt and something sweet like rain, despite the fact that the sky was clear and they could see far into the distance where the mountains disappeared into a line of white haze, they stood in silence for a few minutes, each gazing at different points on the horizon. Hoyle's eyes traced over the peaks and valleys, up and down, the vista looking to him like green waves hardened like glass over which he once imagined he might climb and slide upon like a child in a funhouse. He imagined walking beneath the trees and hearing the creaking of the trunks and boughs and the sharp and echoing snap of fallen branches. He imagined the rough texture of pine bark that left a dusty residue on his fingers, and the constant chill of the few maple trees like dirt just below the frost line, feeling now both energized and saddened by the view, a sort of frantic melancholy that had grown over the years since his father died and that tightened his muscles, and seemed birthed by a strange belief that if he closed his eyes even once this astounding beauty would vanish into a flat table of nothing. He remembered sitting beside his father in this same spot, sometimes with his father's arm around his shoulder, feeling excited as he listened to his father talk about the different sorts of trees and how to recognize them by the shapes of the their leaves, and all the plants, and which were safe to eat, and the dozens of types of animals in the woods and their habits and how to find them.

"It's beautiful," Diane said. "I feel as if I'm floating in a balloon."

"Here, try this." Hoyle sat on the granite, feeling the warmth of the stone through the seat of his pants. "Lie flat on your back and look straight up."

Diane lay beside him, separated by a few inches. "Oh my gosh. It gives me vertigo," she said.

"I used to lie here when I was a kid and daydream I was taking off in a rocket like Neil Armstrong. It's really amazing at night when there's no moon. You feel as if you're spinning in the stars." He heard Diane laugh through her nose, but didn't look at her, feeling awkward about her proximity. He thought about moving away, and felt ashamed. Mustering his courage, and turning his head, he saw she was looking at him as if she were trying to peer into his ear to read his thoughts.

"You know you haven't really kissed me since that night outside the restaurant," she said. "Is it because you don't find me attractive?"

Hoyle could smell something sour, like old coffee on her breath. "No, nothing like that. You're a beautiful woman."

"Then why don't you kiss me?"

Hoyle didn't know why kissing her seemed wrong and a mistake, and rose on an elbow so that his shadow fell across her, and gazed at her, taking in her eyes and lips and breasts. He liked the look of her, and felt aroused by the softness of her flesh and the thought of touching the thin layer of fat that covered her muscles, but couldn't shake the feeling that kissing her seemed almost perverse. She was looking at him now in a way he didn't like, as if she were steeling herself against punishment.

"Smile at me," he said. "Don't look so sad."

Diane did as she was told, but moved only her lips. Her eyes remained unchanged and continued to express the same amount of vulnerability and childlike fear.

When he kissed her, bending quickly so that their front teeth at first hit against each other, he closed his eyes and, ignoring his misgivings, pressed his lips hard against hers. Feeling a surge of desire as she opened her mouth, and pressing his tongue against hers, he moved a hand along the side of her stomach and ribcage, feeling the warmth of her flesh and how it slid over bone beneath her shirt. He reached upward, feeling the contours of her bra, and hesitated a moment before pressing the edge of his thumb against the softness of her breast, surprised by how greatly it fueled his desire to see her naked and caress her body.

She said: "I like the way you kiss me, and how you touch me."

Hoyle said nothing as he twirled a strand of her hair around a forefinger, glad to see the sadness gone from her eyes.

"It's tender and forceful at the same time," she said. "Like you're hungry for me, but would take great care not to harm me. Like you would protect me. It makes me feel safe."

After another half hour, during which they lay on their backs and watched a turkey buzzard soaring on an updraft over the mountain like a kite, they remounted the horses and began the return trip home, the horses clearly tired and moving slower now and more awkwardly, sometimes stumbling over rocks as they headed downhill. Twice, Hoyle halted, giving them a rest and pointing out areas where he and his father used to trek in search of game.

The air grew hotter the farther they descended, and felt almost steamy on the last leg of the path so that their shirts were rimmed by sweat by the time they reached the paddock. Back at the barn, where the other bay stood in the shade near the entrance with its head held high and whinnying in greeting, Hoyle untacked the horses, dragging the saddles and blankets off of them, which he slung over the fence to dry, before hosing them down and letting them loose to roll in the dust and graze in the field. Afterwards, and after Diane giggled at how the horses wriggled on their backs as they rolled, she and Hoyle sat on the porch drinking sweet tea, Diane repeating how much she enjoyed the ride and felt invigorated by it.

"Teach me how to shoot," she said.

"Right now?"

"Yes. I feel so full of energy. I don't want to sit around doing nothing. Will you?"

So Hoyle retrieved the .22 his father gave him he kept in a chest in his bedroom with the other guns, and a piece of paper from a drawer in the kitchen, and led her to the other side of the barn past the manure pile to a small clearing before a copse of trees. Tacking the paper onto one of the trunks, and backing away about fifty feet, he showed her how to hold and aim the rifle, telling her to press the stock against her shoulder and sight along the barrel and not to hold her elbows so far from her body. She held the thing as if it were a spear, not seeming to understand what he was saying, and she meant to thrust it into the tree, but he showed her how to cock it regardless, telling her to fire.

"Ouch! That hurts," she cried when the rifle recoiled against her.

"That's because you weren't pressing it against your shoulder like I told you. Just imagine what it would have felt like if this were a shotgun or something with a real kick. You'd really be hurting."

"Like this?" she asked, raising the rifle.

"Yeah, a little bit tighter." He again told her to lower her elbows, and to take her time aiming and to squeeze the trigger, not jerk it.

She fired ten shots in all, never hitting the target, but was smiling when she handed the rifle to him.

"I could get used to this," she said. "Let's see you."

Hoyle raised the rifle, surprised by how small it seemed in his hands. He hit the center of the paper with his first shot, and five more times in succession, liking how she looked at him with admiration.

Later, she having suggested they cook dinner together, they drove to the nearest food mart for supplies, a small grocery store and gas station owned by a family he'd known his entire life, Hoyle driving his pickup, for some reason feeling embarrassed to be seen in her Mercedes, where they bought an onion and pepper and ham for omelets, a couple of bottles of white wine, and a homemade pecan pie for dessert. At home, they sat again on the porch drinking the wine and enjoying the relative coolness of the gloaming before heading inside to the kitchen where they worked side-by-side until Hoyle told her to take a seat and allow him to do the cooking. Diane switched on an old radio on the counter and lit a candle she found in a drawer, attaching it to a saucer with melted wax and setting it on the table.

"Who taught you how to cook?" she asked.

Hoyle was beating eggs in a bowl when he turned to look at her and was struck by how beautiful and delicate and finely made she seemed in the candlelight like a Christmas ornament as she smiled at him through hair falling over one eye and stroked his cat which had jumped in her lap, the cat's back rising up under her hand. "My mother," he said. "She couldn't abide men who didn't know how. Said it was as foolish as not knowing how to swim. She couldn't figure why someone wouldn't want to master a task that was essential to living."

After eating, then washing the dishes together, she washing, he drying, they returned to the front porch where they finished the first bottle of wine and half of the second. The night smelled of coming rain, and the thick air seemed to push upon the porch light like a weight of water on a bubble. Hoyle liked the feeling, felt cloistered and isolated by it, and inched closer to Diane, throwing his arm around her. When they kissed again, she moving toward him the split second before he decided to, he did not hesitate this time, cupping and fondling her breasts. He held her close, squeezing her and relishing how she moaned when he pinched them and kissed her neck.

"I know you won't hurt me. I know you won't," she said, as she took him by the hand and led him upstairs, looking back at him and smiling the entire way.

Robert Boisvert

PART TWO

He felt guilty the next morning, a sort of tight ball of anxiety at the bottom of his ribcage that seemed to suck up everything around it, leaving him feeling spent and out of breath and in need all the time of inhaling deeply and holding the lungful of air, as if to give his heart time to resuscitate. Eventually, though, over the next several weeks, he grew accustomed to the feeling as it arose often when he saw Diane for the first time after an absence, either when she was brewing coffee downstairs in the mornings or cooking their dinner at her house, or when he met her at a restaurant for a drink, telling himself she was a grown woman who knew what she wanted and could take care of herself.

Thus it was a welcome distraction when he began working long hours for Bob Hager, a contactor who drove a Range Rover outfitted with chrome rims and racing tires, and threatened his workers with violence, especially the Latinos, when he grew angry with them, but who paid top dollar when he eventually did pay. The job was a big one, installing paneling in a library, dining room, and gaming room and hanging crown molding throughout an eight thousand square foot house Bob was building for a wealthy somebody from Raleigh on the side of a mountain about twenty miles east of Asheville, and would require him taking on Langston and Thurmond Williams, two brothers he'd worked with on and off for a dozen years since they moved to the area from the coast. He met the men at the site on the first day of the job, finding them sitting on the tailgate of their pickup, sipping coffee from McDonalds and chatting with two men from a crew hired to hang drywall.

"Man, you looking way too chipper for this early in the morning," Langston said, shaking his head. "You need to scowl a little, or something." Langston was the older brother. Both of them looked as if they spent a good deal of time exercising with weights.

The men began working in the foyer and entrance area where two curving staircases led to the second floor, and where they set up wheeled scaffolding to reach the twenty foot ceilings. Hoyle had agreed to install a three tiered molding—crown, cornice, and dentil molding laid over or under each other—in the entrance way, living room, and dining room, and something less elaborate in all the other rooms. Setting up a staging area just outside the main entrance where they placed the workhorses and power saws, they began measuring and cutting the sixteen foot sections of molding, Hoyle cutting the angles himself, having learned from experience it was best not to trust anyone else, having seen men leave a sixteenth of an inch, or even eighth of an inch gap between boards rather than starting anew, which he could never understand.

They worked well over the first three days, falling into a groove, Langston entertaining them by telling stories about some of the clients they'd recently worked for, like the one woman who hired them to clean out and haul away junk from a garage and guest house who got mad at them because they weren't willing to accept as payment the junk

Robert Boisvert

itself. "You know? Like her dented up shit was somehow worth more than anyone else's dented up shit," he said. "I'm like, 'Lady, we're taking it to the dump. Why would we want it?'" He shook his head. "Rich folk are weird." But on the fourth day, just as they were hanging the first piece of the three tier of molding, Bob strolled into the entrance area, his hands on his hips, saying the molding looked good, and that it would look even better in the gaming room and library, as if that was part of their agreement.

Hoyle left the brothers to finish nailing. "What are you talking about, Bob? That's not what we agreed. We agreed to place the eight inch crown in the gaming room and library."

A big man with fat, red hands and slicked, gray hair, Bob looked at Hoyle as if he were a dunce. "No. Everything down here gets the tiered molding, except the bathrooms and kitchen. The eight inch goes upstairs."

Hoyle wondered if the man were trying to joke with him. "Bob, you know that's not right."

"I don't know anything of the sort. That's what we agreed on."

"Bob, you know it's not true. We went from room to room and talked about it. I took notes."

"Well, you must have crappy handwriting because you got it wrong."

Now Hoyle felt frustrated and embarrassed, knowing the brothers behind him had stopped working and were watching them. "I bought the molding based on our agreement."

"So return it. What's the big deal? I fronted you some money to buy it. Bring it back."

Hoyle was shaking his head. "But the tiered molding is going to cost me a lot more money and take a lot longer to install."

Bob held up both hands to signal he was done talking. "Look, Hoyle, shit. That's the job. You don't want it, I'll find someone else." And he walked past him toward the rear of the house.

Hoyle complained about his treatment to Diane, saying he couldn't believe Bob was trying to cheat him. By now, and despite his occasional feelings of guilt and anxiety, they were seeing each other nearly every day, Hoyle liking most how they settled down into an evening, snuggling on a couch to watch TV. Oftentimes, he felt as if he were existing in one of those dreams in which he knew he was dreaming and was happily in bed asleep, knowing there remained several more hours until morning.

"Don't you have a contract?" she asked.

"A general contract," he said. "You know, a certain price for the installation of crown molding. But nothing that spells out the exact type of molding."

"Well, I guess now you know you need to make it more specific."

Hoyle grew confounded every time he thought about the incident, the motivation of the man not making any sense to him. "But why would he lie like that? Why not just straight up ask for a lower price? What's the point?" He also couldn't quite figure why Diane laughed, and what she meant by, "My sweet man."

Hoyle finished the entrance area and ordered more molding to outfit the rooms as Bob specified, deciding it would do no good to fight him, and that he couldn't afford to lose the job. It took another week and a half for the molding to arrive, and cost him an extra twelve hundred dollars. He remained perturbed about and felt humiliated by the situation, and wasn't looking forward to picking up the molding. Preparing to leave the house one morning, his keys in one hand, a piece of toast in the other, he was fantasizing about Bob admitting his deceitfulness and making amends when he passed the entrance to the living room and was startled to see Christine asleep on the couch, laying on her side in a fetal position.

The sight of her filled him with both joy and sadness. Moving quietly, and sidestepping any floorboards he knew would squeak, he sat on a chair opposite her and watched her sleep. He stared at her, moving his eyes from her hair and cheeks and hands beneath her head and shoulders and elbows and hip bone and knees and feet until he felt as if he might cry. The sight of her seemed then almost painfully perfect in its representation of love, like a statue created via the dictates of his desires and sensibilities he wanted to reach out and touch, but didn't dare for fear of being caught and decried as a vandal.

Again moving carefully, and glancing back at her every other step to be sure he wasn't disturbing her sleep, he returned to the kitchen where he phoned Langston and told him he wouldn't be able to make it to the job today, taking pride in telling him his daughter was sick and needed his help. Afterwards, he turned down the volume of his phone, just in case someone tried calling, then brewed coffee and checked the refrigerator and cabinets to be sure he had enough food to prepare her a large breakfast when she awoke. Eggs, bread, pancake mix, syrup, bacon, orange juice. He only wished he possessed fresh fruit, and for a moment wondered if he should run to the store.

The waiting was hardest, sitting at the kitchen table, his elbows on his knees, and harkening for any sound of her waking. He could feel his anxiousness burrowing like moles in his shoulders. He considered leaving by the back door and killing time by feeding the horses, but didn't dare move, wanting to be almost the first thing she saw when she awoke and to be able to answer if she called out, and for her not to need to search for him. So he remained in the kitchen, remembering a time when she was two years old and sick with fever and how he held her throughout the night, cooling her head with washcloths and walking her when she cried.

He also remembered the day she was born, and the first moment he saw her. Then a birthday, either her first or second. Then a day at the beach on the Outer Banks. But the incompleteness of the memories, coupled with the fact that he could recall only snippets, and that there wasn't more to recall, left him feeling like a fraud and as if he were rifling through the snapshots in someone else's wallet and passing them off as his own. He stared at the floor and concentrated instead on the feeling itself, tonguing it like a canker.

When Christine awoke about forty-five minutes later, and he heard her coughing, Hoyle was scrubbing the countertops with a powdered cleanser so that the room smelled strongly of ammonia. He wiped his hands on a cloth and tossed the cloth and sponge and cleanser under the sink when he heard her shuffle from the living room to the bathroom at the end of the front hall, and stood with his backside against the counter, waiting.

She appeared in the entranceway looking tired and out of sorts, her fine hair chorded in oily clumps hanging in front of her eyes. "I didn't think you'd be here," she said.

Hoyle couldn't figure if she was disappointed. "I took the day off when I saw you," he said. "What time did you get here?"

Christine shook her head. "I don't know. Late. I hope you don't mind."

Hoyle now detected something else which caused him to dismiss the question of disappointment. Taking in her bedraggled and slumped form, and hearing her voice, he sensed a misery in her that filled the air like body odor which she did not attempt to mask. "No. Never," he said. "Are you hungry? I have coffee ready. And I can make you eggs or pancakes. Whatever you want."

"I'm not really hungry."

"When's the last time you ate? You should eat something." Hoyle was taken aback by how she now looked at him and the mix of desire and gratitude and fear. Stepping forward, and pulling out a chair, he said, "Come on. Sit down."

The way Christine hesitated, then almost fell forward into the chair, as if she were diving into the sea on a hot day, caused him to feel as if his heart were being wrung like the sponge tossed beneath the sink. They did not speak while he poured her coffee and set out cream and sugar and cooked her scrambled eggs, bacon, and toast.

Christine attempted to smile at him when he placed the plate of food in front of her. He did not expect her to eat much, and wasn't offended when she took two bites of eggs and a bite of toast and pushed it away and lit a cigarette. She sat hunched in her chair, her shoulders looking as if they might at any moment toss out the first filaments of a cocoon.

"Are you alright?" he asked.

She did not move and didn't answer for a moment, the cigarette smoke curling up and writhing around her. Because her hair hung in front of her face, and because she was hunching her shoulders, he did not realize she was crying until he heard her sniffle.

"I'm tired, Daddy," she said, each word wriggling out of her mouth and seeming to plop onto the floor like a slug.

Hoyle knew she meant more than physical weariness, that there was something dark and grotesque contained within her complaint. Standing and taking the cigarette from her and tossing it into the sink, he led her upstairs to the bedroom he used as a child and she used the few times she stayed here. The room smelled musty and baked by the sun. On the wall hung a poster of an all female rock band, its corners curling.

"I haven't changed it since the last time you were here," he said.

He pulled back the covers and laid her in bed. She rolled onto her side.

"Just sleep," he said. "Sleep as long as you want."

"Okay," she said.

"Don't worry about a thing. I'll be here when you wake up."

"Okay."

Before leaving, he opened two windows and pulled the shades, the shades giving the room a golden glow, as if illuminated by candlelight.

Downstairs, he busied himself finishing cleaning the kitchen, then by feeding the horses and cleaning the barn. Tossing clumps of manure into a wheelbarrow, and dumping them on the pile behind the barn, then sweeping the floorboards, the dirt and dust rising in the air and shimmering like bits of glass in the few rays of sun penetrating the patched roof, he thought about the darkness contained in the word "tired" and what it entailed. The truth of what she meant sat like a sealed blockhouse in front of him he did not wish to explore, or even look upon, the idea of it, even its simple existence, filling him with a sadness and trepidation that felt like boiling water in his gut. Remembering the ugliness of her boyfriend, Shawn, and the sight of Christine in dirty clothes, he began to imagine the difficulty she may have encountered grasping the mere necessities of life, and felt a shame and sorrow and embarrassment for her sake so great he dropped the broom and left the barn and walked into the field toward the path to the Skulls.

He did not wander far, only to the edge of the path, but soon felt better, having resolved by way of a simple statement, "It will be better," and to comfort and envelop her like a baby in a blanket. Returning to the house, and grabbing a piece of paper and a pen, he began making a list of the food and other items he would need to buy for her, including clothes and shoes. He then pulled out his phone and called Diane.

He told her Christine had come to stay with him and that he was sorry he was going to have to cancel dinner that night because she wasn't doing too well.

The silence on the other end of the line told him she wasn't pleased.

"Hello?" he asked.

"I'm here. I'm just wondering how I can help. Maybe I can bring over some food, or talk to her, girl-to-girl."

Hoyle was surprised by the offer and appreciative, but suspected Christine might feel self-conscious in front of Diane and not want to stay. Plus, he was feeling selfish and didn't want to share his daughter's attentions with anyone. He told Diane he would call her that night.

Grabbing the list, and stepping outside again, he climbed into his truck, feeling purposeful and empowered. Driving faster than normal, not wanting to be away from the house too long, he sped to the nearest Walmart about twenty minutes away where he purchased food and clothes, including two pairs of jeans, each in a different size, just in case, several T-shirts, underwear, socks, and a pair of flip flop type sandals, plus a bar of perfumed soap, a toothbrush, shampoo, and conditioner. Buying the clothes took longer than expected, since he felt too embarrassed to ask for help, and tried sizing his purchases by gauging the clothes women shoppers were wearing or selecting.

But Christine was still asleep when he returned home about two hours later, laying so still in bed he panicked for a moment wondering if she were breathing. Back downstairs, where he opened all the windows, he set about cleaning the rest of the house, sweeping and washing the floors and dusting the furniture. He then began making a large pot of chicken soup from a recipe his mother taught him, chopping carrots and celery and onions, and hoping the aroma would waft upstairs and cause her to feel secure and more at home.

Christine awoke in the middle of the afternoon and trod downstairs so slowly Hoyle wondered if she were reconsidering at each step returning to bed. Her face looked puffy and pale when she appeared in the kitchen. Shuffling toward the table, and dropping into chair as if her tail end were magnetized, she eyed the pot of soup still simmering on the stove, then the bags of clothes and toiletries on the counter. Her frailness caused Hoyle to hesitate speaking for fear she might crumble like a sandcastle.

"Are you hungry?" he asked.

She shook her head. "No." Her voice was hoarse and soft.

"You should eat something. How about a little soup?"

Christine again shook her head and looked as if she might throw up. "Do you have any more coffee?"

Hoyle began to worry about her lack of appetite, and wondered if she were sick. "No, but I can make some." He moved to the coffee maker.

Christine lit a cigarette and sat now with her arms tight around her body, as if she were cold, and despite the heat of the day. They said nothing for a few minutes, the only sound in the room the hiss and drip of the brewing coffee.

"I got these for you," Hoyle said, carrying the bags to the table. "I hope they fit."

Christine peered at him through the cigarette smoke, one eye half shut. She then craned her neck to look into the bags without touching them. "What is it?"

"A few clothes. Toiletries. A toothbrush and stuff. I thought you might want to get cleaned up."

She looked at him.

"I don't mean you need to or anything," he said, feeling foolish. "I just thought if you wanted to."

Christine smiled and nodded her head. "Thank you."

Hoyle poured a cup of coffee and placed it in front of her, pushing aside the bags. He then retrieved cream and sugar and a tea spoon before sitting opposite her. "Are you okay?" he asked, hoping she wasn't offended by his prying.

She stared at the coffee and shrugged her shoulders. He could see tears welling in her eyes.

Robert Boisvert

"I can't do this anymore," she said. "It's too hard. I'm not using like I used to, like Momma thinks I am. I'm using a little bit again, but not a lot. But I know I will, eventually. I know it's only a matter of time before I give in. I see the ones who are using a lot all around me all the time, twitching and picking at their acne and scabby skin. I smell their stink, the foulness of them and the stench of their rotting teeth, and I think: that's going to be me.

"I remember the old feeling of being a ghost in this world. Like I'd died but was too heavy still to float to heaven and too light to drop into hell. Instead, I was a ghost who couldn't touch or grab hold onto anything like I was made up of nothing more than wind passing over or through everything in the world." The tears began to roll down her cheeks, streaking her dirty face. "The only time it was bearable was when I was high, and that's because nothing then existed outside my brain. Nothing to worry about. It was as if I was living then in a universe bordered by the backs of my eyeballs and the inside of my skull in which stars and suns and planets of green grass and blue water floated like balloons. I don't know that I was happy like I remember, but I didn't feel lost and without substance.

"But afterwards, when I was coming down, every time it was like those terrible, terrible moments when you realize you might be wrong about your opinion of yourself, when you realize someone doesn't love you, and maybe for valid reasons, or you hear people laughing at you. It was crushing, this weight of the real world landing on me, and painful like someone throwing the blinds up on the last legs of a binge to this brilliant reality. I saw people going to work in the morning, fresh and clean from a shower. They were purposeful and energetic, striding the sidewalks, sometimes sneering at me, or worse, ignorant of my presence.

"And so I'd become frantic, even before the physical cravings kick in. I'd want more than anything to get back to my own universe, and would do almost anything to get there.

Anything. Except I knew it wasn't real, this universe inside my head, and that these things I'd do to get back there had consequences. And I saw myself doing these awful, awful things and I'd hate myself and knew I was undeserving of every breath I took and was wicked and cursed.

"I don't want it, Daddy. I feel myself slipping, but I don't want to go back there. It's too hard and I can't do it anymore."

When she finished speaking, and stared down at a point on the table, as if wishing even now to vanish into that other universe she described, Hoyle waited a moment before standing. It was painful to hear her speak about such things, but he was feeling then a surge of love for her greater than any he'd ever felt, a frenetic emotion that seemed to impel and knit with his muscles, increasing their strength. Stepping over to her, moving slowly for fear of spooking her or causing her to believe she in any way upset him, and seeing how she tensed her shoulders and arms, as if expecting to be hit, he leaned down and kissed her on the top of her head, smelling at the same time her unwashed hair and rankness, and said, "You may stay here as long as you like. Forever, if you want," words and actions that seemed to surprise her by the way they caused her to sob and grab onto him and hold tight, as if his arms were the only things preventing her from melting into a puddle on the floor.

Hoyle stayed home from work the next day as well, telling the brothers his daughter was sicker than he at first thought, and that he might need another day too, he couldn't tell. Sitting in the kitchen, and drinking coffee, he felt happy and content listening to the sounds of his daughter rising and showering, of doors opening and closing and the hum of water in the pipes in the walls, feeling then as if he were existing in a cartoon in which the house itself was happy and bouncing up and down on its foundation like a puppy. When Christine emerged from upstairs, combing her wet

Robert Boisvert

hair and wearing the clothes he bought, he smiled and said, "You look good. I'm glad they fit."

Christine seemed shy and hid her smile, saying, "They're a little big. I might need to borrow a belt."

After breakfast, during which she ate eggs, bacon, and two helpings of toast with strawberry jam, they walked outside where Christine stood on the lower railing of the fence and petted one of the bays. Hoyle asked if she wanted to ride, but she said, no, she was still a little tired, and instead they strolled through the field toward the path, Christine occasionally bending to pick a flower.

They did not talk about anything of consequence. Mostly, memories of Hoyle's childhood, his daughter asking whether the place had changed much from when he was a child, and about her grandmother and grandfather, and what he used to do to keep himself occupied, Hoyle telling her about the overnight hunting trips he and his father used to take into the mountains and how much he enjoyed them.

He said: "I remember standing beside him and looking out over the valleys and mountains and thinking how beautiful the world was and how much more beautiful it could be, and feeling as if more and more of it were going to spring up from the ground like flowers and trees.

"We should do that," he said, feeling excited.

"Hunting?"

"No, not hunting. Just pack the horses and ride off into the mountains for a few days. You wouldn't believe the feel of the place, how the smell of pine seems to infuse your body and give it all this strength."

She was smiling, but shook her head. "I don't know if I could. I'd probably wimp out after only a few hours."

"Oh, of course you could do it. You and I up there? It'd be great. At night around a campfire. The stars are so bright they're like little lamps hanging from a ceiling, like you could reach up and flick them."

She laughed. "I'd probably get eaten by a bear."

"Nah, no bear's going to bother you. You kidding? Just holler and shout and chunk him with a couple of rocks like my dad and I used to do, that's all."

"You used to see bear?"

Hoyle felt a measure of pride remembering his first sight of a bear and how he felt more fascination than any amount of fear as he crouched next to his father, his shoulder pressed against the man's ribcage, and watched the sow snuffling through the forest.

"She's looking for acorns, trying to fatten up before hibernation," he heard his father say.

"Do you think she knows we're here," Hoyle remembered asking. He remembered wanting to have his father throw a lasso around its neck and to grip the fur on its back and ride it through the woods.

"Probably not. She'd have skittered if she'd have seen or heard us. But don't worry. You really only have watch out if you see one with her cubs. That's when you have to keep your distance and make sure they know you're around."

Hoyle bent and picked a Black Eyed Susan and handed it to Christine. "Sure," he said. "Not often, but every now and then. They're not much more than big, smelly dogs. They don't bother you."

"They smell?" Christine asked, sniffing the flower before adding it to her collection.

"Rank. Musty. You feel it on the back of your throat."

Christine straightened her shoulders as she stared ahead of them. He could see her imagining some scene, perhaps either an encounter with a bear or the two of them on horseback. "You really think I could do it?"

He nudged her with an elbow. "Come on. Sure I do. I don't think you'd have any problems."

The feelings of happiness and contentment continued through the evening as Hoyle cooked a dinner of spaghetti and meatballs, something he remembered her liking as a child. They ate in the dining room, Hoyle using his mother's best plates, and afterwards drank beer on the porch.

"I was thinking I could try and get my old job back. Or maybe I could find one as a waitress," she said. "But I'd first have to get my car from Momma's. I mean, it's not really mine. It's the one she let me use."

Hoyle had been listening to the owl that roosted in the barn, and didn't want to think about her mother, or leaving, or getting a job, or in any way shifting what they now had. "Why?"

"Because I need it to get around. I can't have you driving me everywhere."

"No, I mean why do you want to get a job?"

Christine looked at him as if she didn't understand the question.

"Did you like doing what you did?" he asked. "Or do you think you'd like being a waitress?"

"Not really," she said.

"Then why do it?" He saw she was having difficulty trying to form an answer.

He said: "If it's just to keep busy, I understand. But don't think you have to work, or that I'm expecting you to. There isn't much worse than working a job you hate. I've had a few myself and seen it suck the life out of good men. I'd rather you waited until you found something you really want to do. Or maybe go to school and take some classes at the community college. I mean, there's no point in trying to mend your life by dropping yourself in the same mess you were in, and hoping you can cope better. Right?"

Christine was no longer looking at him. Staring ahead into the darkness, and blinking her eyes to fight off tears, she nodded her head, saying only, "Okay."

Still, he wondered how she would fill her days when he returned to work two days later, having picked up the extra molding and began installing it in the rooms Bob wanted. He didn't want to leave, and worried she might grow bored and make contact with her old friends, looking for something to do to pass the time. That first day, he drove home expecting to be disappointed, and wouldn't have been surprised to find the house empty, but was relieved to see her working in the barn, cleaning out old junk and piling it on the opposite side of the fence. She smiled and waved when she saw him, and wiped the sweat from her brow with the back of a work glove.

"You know, some of this stuff is worth money," she said, pointing with her chin at the pile.

"Oh yeah?"

"Like that old oil lantern. I bet if we cleaned it up we could sell it for a bunch of money. Tourists love this stuff."

Hoyle felt a flood of emotion like warm water swirling between his ribs, hearing her use the word "we." "Sure, let's do it."

Her smile broadened. "Dinner will be ready in about a half hour. I'm making lasagna."

Hoyle also felt relieved when eventually he introduced Christine to Diane. He'd been speaking to Diane every day since Christine arrived, oftentimes more than once, and began dropping by her place during his lunch break, as soon as he returned to work. He missed her more than he expected, and felt an aching desire for her once he saw and held her. But he worried about her franticness and moodiness, one moment talking about plans for their future, the other saying things like, "I know you're going to leave me," and how she would cling to him when he left her house, as if she'd dreamed he was going to be killed in a car crash and was trying to prevent it from coming true.

He hesitated even mentioning Diane to Christine, let alone inviting her to dinner, wondering if it might cause her to feel as if she were crowding him, or as if the other woman might displace her and push her to the wayside. He also wondered if it might cause Christine to miss her mother and prompt her to somehow try to include her in their lives, something Hoyle knew would put an end to their happiness.

But Christine seemed excited about the prospect of meeting one of his friends—that's how Hoyle described Diane—and said she was glad he met a woman he liked. In fact, when Diane arrived for dinner, Christine ushered her in as if she were a favorite and missed aunt, which confused Hoyle. Diane brought with her bottles of red and white wine, and soon the two women were standing in the kitchen and drinking and chatting as they put the finishing touches on the meal, while Hoyle watched from a distance, still bracing for an explosion, as if he were peering at a firecracker whose fuse had fizzled out, and wondered if they were playacting, or if they'd called each other prior to this night and already made introductions.

They ate roast chicken with greens, sweet potatoes, and macaroni and cheese. Afterwards, they ate strawberry rhubarb pie and played UNO and Clue in the living room, games which Hoyle's mother had given him and which he kept stored on the top shelf in the hall closet. Diane did most of the talking, describing and telling funny stories about places she'd visited—Paris, London, New York, the Caribbean—which Hoyle could see fascinated Christine, as she sat in an easy chair with her legs curled beneath her.

"I could see you in New York," Diane said, looking at Christine as if she were appraising a work of art.

Christine looked from her to Hoyle, her eyes wide.

"No, I could," Diane said. "You're just the right age. The bars, the restaurants, the culture. The opportunities. It's a city of dreams."

"Oh, I don't know," Christine said.

"A pretty girl like you? You'd have men eating out of your hand before you knew it."

Hoyle enjoyed hearing the two of them discussing clothes and restaurants, Christine asking lots of questions, and got a little drunk drinking wine and beer so that soon he was telling stories about his daughter as a toddler and how she once copied her mother getting made up one evening by smearing a red magic marker on her cheeks and lips, and how she asked one day in mid-July to, "call up Santa and tell him it's Christmas."

Hoyle enjoyed the next month and a half as if the days were like sweet, hard candy he might roll around in his mouth and suck on at leisure, and would remember them later as some of the best in his life. Twice or three times a week Diane would eat dinner with him and his daughter, staying until late in the night, and kiss him in the porch light, pushing herself against him so that he would grow aroused and not want to let her go. Sometimes he would find her already there, sitting in the kitchen with Christine when he arrived home from work, laughing or talking in earnest, Christine paying close attention. He thought, "This is how it's supposed to be," as if the image of the two women sitting side-by-side fit some divine template from the Old Testament written on goat skin and described in this or that many cubits. Laying in bed, and despite not being a religious man, he would feel the temptation to thank God for his good fortune and pray for its continuance, feeling an anxiety about what seemed too good to be true.

Perfection seemed to have descended and settled on his life like snow, freezing everything in place, even sound. He could smell and feel and taste it all around him: in his sunlit bedroom in which motes of dust seemed to float and pulsate like tiny jellyfish; in the texture and warmth of a wooden hammer handle, worn smooth from years of use and feeling like driftwood; in the indigo and humid evenings when bats would flit overhead and long-legged insects would cling to the screen door, their legs trembling as they reached higher; or in the salty taste of Diane's neck, his lips sliding over the goose bumps and minute hairs on her skin and the chords of muscle beneath them. He felt as if he were drunk all the time, and nearly invulnerable, as if the world were made of marshmallows and pillows so that if he fell he would laugh and remain unharmed.

It wasn't until Shawn first appeared that he remembered his anxiety, and even then figured it would pass. He and Christine were finishing dinner in the kitchen when they heard the pounding beat of his car radio growing louder as his car approached the house, then an abrupt silence as he switched off his car, creating what seemed a vacuum, pulling on their ears. Right away, from the frightened expression on her face, Hoyle knew she recognized the music and who the car belonged to. He walked to the front door and opened it just as Shawn climbed out of his car, a low-riding, late model Honda with an oversized spoiler, and reached the stairs to the porch. Shawn stopped with one foot on the third stair and the other on the second, and smiled.

"Hey, old man, how's it hanging?" He then thrust out his chest, as if he were aping a Nineteenth Century Shakespearean actor, and announced, "I came for my woman."

Christine appeared behind Hoyle, pressing up against him, and peered around his shoulder.

"There you are, honey pie," Shawn said. "Praise the Lord. And look at you looking all fat and clean. Mmm-mmm. Baby, you know how long I've been searching for you? Why, years and years and years. You had me worried, I'll tell you. I swear I cried myself to sleep each night, missing you. I did." He looked at Hoyle. "The girl's got a gift. I mean—" he adopted a stage whisper and winked an eye "—no one can suck a cock like she can."

Hoyle was neither scared nor riled by the man. Watching his antics, and seeing how he swayed on his feet and gazed at them through heavy lidded and glassy eyes, he felt only pity for him, and wished he might be able to hold up a mirror and cause him to see him as the world did. "Why don't you go home, boy," he said. "Sleep it off. She doesn't want anything more to do with you."

Shawn switched his attention to Hoyle, and looked at him like a playful lover. "Boy? Go home?" he said. "Man. Why you teasing me like that? You hoping for a little action too?"

Hoyle could not understand how the man could continue in this manner, acting the fool, certain he would eventually reflect upon and regret his actions. A part of him even wanted to embrace him and say, "That's enough. Let it go."

"Go on, son," he said. "There's nothing here for you."

Shawn placed both feet on the third step. "Or what?"

"I'm calling the sheriff."

Shawn at first looked as if he didn't understand the punch line to a joke. Then his smile broadened. "That's it?"

Hoyle backed up, gesturing for his daughter to go inside. "Good night," he said. "Drive safe."

Shawn climbed onto the porch. He was laughing. "No, really. That's it?"

Hoyle entered the house and shut and locked the door, saying, "I'm calling the sheriff." Pulling his cell phone from a pocket, and dialing 9-1-1, he could hear Shawn on the other side cackling and stomping around, kicking over furniture, and shouting, "Jesus, come on!" Christine had pressed her back against the stair banister and was staring at the door as if she expected a demon to burst through it.

"Yes ma'am," he told the emergency operator, "there's a young man kicking up a fuss on my property and won't leave. Could you send somebody?" The woman asked a few questions about whether the man was armed or had attacked anyone, and took Hoyle's address and said she would dispatch a deputy. Hoyle considered also calling his friend Travis, but figured he was already off duty and that he needn't bother him at home.

"Daddy, get your gun. Please."

Hoyle turned and stared at his daughter. He was surprised to see how scared she was. "Sweetie, it's okay," he said. "He's

Robert Boisvert

just showing off and venting his frustration. There's nothing out there that can't be mended or replaced."

Christine was shaking her head. "You don't understand. You don't know how mean he is. He wants you to hate him. Don't you see? He won't be satisfied until you hate him." She jumped when Shawn kicked the door, shouting, "Come on, old man! Let's play!"

"Daddy," she pleaded. "Please. Get your gun."

Seeing the tears in her eyes, and hearing her voice tremble, Hoyle reached out to embrace her, wanting to calm and reassure her, as he might have if she'd woken from a nightmare; but Christine wriggled away from him and ran upstairs, slamming her bedroom door. Hoyle stood a moment staring after her, wondering if he should follow. It pained him to see her so distraught. But he decided against it, thinking he couldn't force her to realize the truth of the situation, that Shawn would soon leave and that he couldn't affect their lives if they did not allow him to, and that, eventually, she would see it on her own.

Hoyle turned and looked at the front door, thinking of the man on the other side as a little boy throwing a tantrum. Shawn had ceased hollering and kicking things, but Hoyle knew he was still there, probably with an ear to the door, listening. He pictured the man growing disappointed and despondent, his silly looking grin fading as he began to realize the heartlessness and stupidity of his actions. A few more moments passed before Hoyle heard the man shout, "I'll be back," like Arnold Schwarzenegger in the Terminator movies, adding in his own voice, "Motherfucker," then start his car and speed off, gravel hitting the porch.

The sheriff's deputy arrived about twenty minutes later, a young man with a mustache who seemed deflated when he learned Shawn had already left. Hoyle invited him into the kitchen where he served him a glass of iced tea.

"I'd recommend your daughter file a restraining order against the suspect," he said after Hoyle explained what happened. The deputy stood with his right thumb tucked into his holster near his pistol and his other arm leaned against the back of a chair. "We can't really do much against him without that. I mean, we can charge him with destruction of property for breaking one of your chairs, but that isn't going to get him anything but a fine, if that."

Hoyle thanked him, said it sounded like a good idea, and wrote down the man's cell phone number before showing him out.

Upstairs, he listened for a moment outside Christine's bedroom, wondering if he should knock or leave her be. He worried about bothering her, knowing he wouldn't want to be pestered if he were trying to work something out or needed to cry.

"Sweetie, are you alright," he called through the door.

Christine did not respond.

"The deputy was here. He said we should take out a restraining order," he said. "Maybe that's something we could do tomorrow."

He waited another twenty seconds or so, shifting on his feet. Then he returned downstairs to watch TV and call Diane.

Diane said: "The girl's going to need to face these things, these demons from her past. It's part of life. There's never going to be any avoiding it. At least, not as long as she stays around here."

The next day Hoyle called Travis and met him for lunch at a barbecue shack on the outskirts of Asheville where kids in their high school class used to gather on Friday and Saturday nights.

"He's coming back," Travis said, after they carried their plastic baskets filled with pulled pork sandwiches and hushpuppies and their bottles of Coke to a round picnic table covered by a tattered umbrella. "You know that, right? You need to be prepared."

"Maybe he's realized Christine wants nothing to do with him," Hoyle said. He had imagined Shawn sleeping off the drugs or alcohol and ruing his antics.

Travis paused while squirting a barbecue sauce from a plastic bottle onto his sandwich. He stared at Hoyle. "Hoyle, there's no question about his returning. I mean it. You need to be prepared."

Hoyle suspected Travis was being overly cautious, and appreciated the sentiment. "I hear you," he said, despite not fully believing him. He couldn't imagine any man not seeing the truth of the situation, and the pain he might cause.

Travis continued staring.

"I hear you," Hoyle repeated. He lifted the bun off his sandwich and used a plastic fork to scoop coleslaw onto the meat. "So what you're saying is we should definitely file a restraining order."

Travis took a bite of sandwich and wiped his mouth with a paper napkin before responding. "I guess." He shrugged his shoulders. "It certainly can't hurt. I could nail him for violating it, and it might get him thirty days or so. Maybe. If the judge ain't a candy ass. But it won't stop him from coming around again." He popped a hushpuppy into his mouth and washed it down with a swig of Coke.

"There's something seriously wrong with that boy," he continued. "He needs hate like ordinary folks need air or water. I can't tell you how many times we were called to his momma's house because of him fighting. Lots of them fights he didn't win. Got his ass kicked by his brothers or whatever morons his mother was shacked up with. But he never cared. He was just fighting to fight. Like he needed it to keep his heart pumping and blood flowing." He paused again, wiping his hands with another napkin, and sat up straight.

"Get this. One day when he's about, oh I don't know, seventeen or so, he and his friends are out hanging around the old quarry near Georgetown and there's this rattler they come across hiding under a rock. Now they could've just let it be and walked away, but Shawn being the crazy dipshit that he is starts messing with it and poking it with a stick. So of course the thing strikes out and tries to bite him. And what does Shawn do? He hits it with a rock, pretty much killing it, then grabs it and bites it on the head right between the head and neck. I'm not kidding. Like he means to rip the thing in half. Except what happens is he ingests all this venom. Not a whole lot of it but enough so that the doctor in the emergency room tells me his face swelled up like a balloon. So much he thinks the skin's going to burst. And later, when I ask Shawn, he's laying there in the hospital, his face all black and blue like he's been in a prize fight, I ask him why'd you go and do something so stupid? And he smiles, or tries to anyway, and says, 'To show the fucker how it's done.'"

Travis was shaking his head.

"That's Shawn," he said. "That's what you got to be prepared for. The boy is just plain bad, mean through and through. Understand?"

Back at work, having finished the crown molding and working now on the paneling in the library, Hoyle thought about the story, trying to get it clear in his mind, but couldn't ever quite picture the moment when Shawn bit the snake. He could see the snake striking out, and Shawn hitting it with a rock. He could see that clearly. And he could see the aftereffects, Shawn in the hospital with his face like a balloon. But what got him there, the point at which his teeth latched onto the snake's head remained shrouded in a sort of mental fog, mostly because he could not fathom the reason for anyone doing such a thing.

Later, having dropped by Diane's house after work, he repeated the story and asked what she thought about it.

"Oh, that can't be true," she said. "It's ridiculous. He'd have died right there and then. It sounds like one of those urban myths everyone repeats. You know, like the guy who says he knows this guy who flashed his high beams at a passing car, and the passing car turns out to be full of gang members. And they turn around and run him off the road and like ten guys get out and beat him up because flashing your lights is taken as a challenge to them."

"But I don't think Travis would lie," Hoyle said. "That's not like him."

"Well, maybe he's not lying. Maybe he's just exaggerating to help make a point to you. That doesn't mean he's lying, per se."

The point she was making still didn't make sense to Hoyle and caused him to feel less confident about his decision to drive Christine the next morning to the courthouse to file a restraining order. He didn't like courthouses, not after what happened between him and his ex-wife, and walked inside looking around as if he expected to be taken into custody. They were pointed to the office of the Clerk of Superior Court where they waited in line with a group of people who seemed embarrassed or sad or guilty and spoke in whispers, as if the people were attending the funeral of a man they collectively killed, and where the two of them were directed by a fat woman in a lime green dress to fill out a number of forms, including one on which Christine needed to detail how Shawn abused her.

Hoyle said: "Write down that he's harassing you and threatening to break in where you're living, and that he's said he's going to return. Don't leave anything out."

But Christine took the form to a corner chair and turned her body in such a way to prevent him from seeing what she was writing, afterwards telling him, "It's not important," when he asked what she put down.

When they finally were brought before a judge, a thin older man wearing half glasses on the end of a nose as pointy as an arrowhead, having waited much longer than Hoyle anticipated so that he grew more nervous and needed to call the brothers and instruct them on what to do until he arrived in the afternoon, the judge read the form and the others for what seemed a longer time than was necessary before saying, "Is this true?" He was looking at Christine over the tops of his glasses.

Christine nodded her head.

"Have you talked to the police?" the judge asked.

"No sir," she said.

The judge glanced again at the forms and pursed his lips. "I understand." He looked at Hoyle. "And who's this?"

"He's my father," Christine said.

Hoyle was wondering what was written on the form and didn't understand what the judge meant by, "I'm glad to hear that."

"She's living with you now, young man?" the judge asked.

"Yes sir," Hoyle said. He wasn't sure why he added, "She just moved in a couple of months ago."

"Good," the judge said. He picked up a pen. "Young lady, I'm granting what's called an Ex parte Temporary Protective Order. It's good for only ten days. I'm also setting a hearing for a Domestic Violence Protective Order that will be good for a year. You'll have to come back here for a hearing. But don't worry. I'm pretty sure it's only a formality and we won't have any problem granting it." The judge then paused a moment to write on the forms. "Now, if you see this fellow you immediately call the police. No hesitation. You understand?"

"Yes sir," Christine said.

"Good. Good luck to you. And you, young man," he said to Hoyle, "keep her close." The judge then banged his gavel, handed the forms to an assistant, and said, "Next."

Hoyle felt relieved and a sort of pride in having accomplished something meaningful, liking how the judge seemed to have awarded him an official seal of approval, telling Christine on the ride back to the house, "Don't you worry. You'll see. Everything will be just fine." But Christine kept quiet, and withdrew and grew more sullen over the next days and weeks, as if she were mad at him and everyone else she came into contact with. She took to eating her meals in front of the TV and no longer performed many chores around the house, often leaving dishes in the sink with her cigarette butts stabbed out on them.

One night, while she, Hoyle, and Diane were playing crazy eights after dinner, and Hoyle was telling a story about the first time Christine ever saw a kitten, and didn't know the word for kitten, calling it instead a "baby meow," she threw down her cards and stomped into the kitchen. Hoyle stared after her, trying to figure out what went wrong, then glanced at Diane.

"I don't know," she said. "I think she's just now figuring out no one else can solve her problems. Leave her be," she added, when Hoyle made to stand up.

But Hoyle followed Christine into the kitchen, finding her standing by the sink and smoking a cigarette.

"What's wrong?" he asked.

"I hate those stories," she said, flicking ash into the sink.

"I'm sorry. I didn't mean anything. They're just sort of an expression of how much I care for you. I won't tell them anymore."

"How much you care?" The look she gave him felt as if she were pressing the cigarette into his skin. "Baby meow. Ain't it cute? How about when my bike was stolen when I was six and Momma spanked me, saying it was my fault for riding it to my friend's house? Why don't you tell that story? Or how about when I was beat up in seventh grade by a group of girls for being fat? Or how about when Momma's boyfriend, Leroy, kept trying to kiss me one night when I was thirteen and Momma was passed out drunk, and I had to lock myself in the bathroom to get away from him? Why don't you tell those stories, Daddy?" She pulled a face as if pretending to be sad. "Oh yeah, 'cause you weren't around to see them." She threw her cigarette into the sink and ran upstairs.

Hoyle stared at the spot she'd vacated, his face burning with shame, and feeling his heart beating high in his chest and as if his bones were melting and he might at any moment shrivel into a puddle on the linoleum. He was surprised to hear Diane behind him, standing beneath the lintel.

"She has no right," she said. "She's only striking out against the one person who loves her because she hasn't found the courage to look at herself."

Hoyle didn't comment before following Christine up the stairs. He knocked on her door, heard nothing, and entered anyway, finding her lying on her stomach on the bed.

"Go away," she said.

Hoyle closed the door behind him, closing it as if he were trying not to wake her, and walked to the bed. He wanted to sit and maybe stroke her back or head, but remained standing.

"Baby, you have to understand," he said. "I tried to see you as much as I could. Your mother, I don't know why, we shared custody for a while after we split and I would see you a couple of times a week. But your mother hated me in a way I couldn't understand and couldn't change. A hatred I couldn't account for. And when our divorce was finalized, she took me to court and sued for sole custody. She told terrible lies. Said I beat her, and drank, and never paid child support, and even hinted that I molested you. I tried to tell the judge the truth, that I never once laid a hand on her, and didn't drink, and always paid your mother cash. That she had demanded cash, and that's why I didn't have any cancelled checks or records to show that I paid. And that I would never ever do anything to hurt you. That I loved you more than anything. But the judge believed her, and granted her custody. And so your mother would only let me see you every once in a while. And if I did show up

68   Robert Boisvert

uninvited, she'd threaten to call the sheriff on me, and tell me I'd never see you again.

"But you've got to believe me, I wanted to see you, and loved you, and thought about you every day. It wasn't as if I was avoiding you. Those few times I'd see you, like the week or so in the summer or around Christmas, I can't tell you how much I looked forward to them. And I knew that one day you'd understand, and everything would turn out all right, and you'd come back into my life. Like you are now. I swear it."

Christine waited a moment after he finished before lifting herself on her elbows. She didn't look at him and stared ahead at the headboard. "Do you know what I thought about when Leroy was chasing me and I locked myself in the bathroom?" she asked.

Hoyle braced himself for the answer. "No, what?"

"You," she said. "Not Leroy and his stinking aftershave. Or Momma passed out on the couch. I thought about how much I hated you and how I wanted you to have to watch me die, like in a car crash or something." She lowered herself again so that what she said next was muffled by the pillow. "Not everything in life turns out alright, Daddy. That's what fathers are for."

Hoyle stared at nothing. For the next several days, whether at work or Diane's or home with Christine, he operated as if he were an automaton, as if carnival goers had dropped coins into a slot to see him saw wood or turn on a TV or fix dinner. The words his daughter spoke seemed to have bumped him from the rails of time. He felt as if he were trapped in a tunnel and could not see ahead through the mossy blackness to the future. Might the ground fall away in one step? Two? A thousand? He couldn't tell. All he knew was that now the seconds, minutes, days, years of his past he could hear piling up and crashing into each other like the cars of a train were poised to come tumbling over him, pinning him beneath an unbearable weight of guilt and shame.

He told Diane he could not figure where he went wrong. "It all seemed so right at the time," he said.

Diane was massaging his shoulders in the den of her home, having taken off his work boots and brought him a beer. "Hush now. You didn't do anything wrong," she said. "She's just trying to blame you for her mistakes. Most everyone has a difficult childhood. My father might as well have been living elsewhere, the amount of affection he gave me, or even talked to me. That doesn't mean I became a drug addict."

Hoyle could already feel the pressure of his past weighing down on him, pushing on the top of his head. "But I failed her. I know I failed her."

Diane dug deep into his muscles, causing him to wince. "You make me so angry when you say such things. She's twenty-one, for goodness sake. It's high time she stood up on her own two feet and fought her own battles. Why is it you're responsible for her failures?"

Hoyle was picturing Christine when she was twelve or thirteen, looking plump and awkward in ill-fitting clothes and spiky hair with purple highlights. The image shocked and shamed him. "Maybe it was because I always thought she was beautiful and figured other people would see the same thing."

Events only began moving forward once more for Hoyle about a week later when Shawn appeared again on a Monday night. He was sitting alone in the kitchen while Christine watched TV in the living room when he heard the booming beat of his car stereo. Pushing himself from the table, and moving to the front door, he found Christine holding onto the door jamb between the living room and hallway, her face pressed against the wood.

"Call 9-1-1. Right now. Go on," he said when she hesitated, realizing and regretting that they were only a few of the handful of sentences he'd said to her all evening.

Robert Boisvert

Outside, he descended the porch steps to where Shawn was leaning against his car and grinning.

"Ready to play for real, old man?"

"We've called 9-1-1," Hoyle said, stopping about ten feet from the other man, and feeling more anxious and high strung this time than the last. "We've taken out a restraining order. You're going to be arrested if you're still around here when they get here."

Shawn pushed himself off the car and threw his arms up into the air. "See? Now there you go again. That's so lame." He stopped and looked over Hoyle's shoulder and waved at Christine in the doorway. "Hey baby. Almost ready for me to take you home?" Then to Hoyle he said, "Do you have any pictures of her? Because I'm thinking of taking some pictures of her. You seem like a sentimental guy, the type of guy who would cherish that sort of thing. Because here's what I'm thinking. I'm thinking of taking some intimate photos of her, then maybe letting my friends take some. Would you like a few? Because I could send them around to you. Or maybe I'll post them on the Internet, let everyone see how sweet your daughter is. How about that?"

The anger in Hoyle's belly felt like a scrabbling rat trying to set itself free. Staring at Shawn's boyish face and trying to find in it any hint as to the reason for his seeming intransigence, he said, "Why are you doing this? It's a beautiful evening. Look around you." He turned and pointed to his daughter, his voice rising. "Look at her. She's just a girl. Why aren't you willing to acknowledge what's right in front of your eyes?" Then, before he could stop himself, and with the same hand he used to point at Christine, he swung with all his might and hit Shawn on the chin. Shawn stumbled backwards and fell to the ground.

"Daddy," he heard Christine scream.

Shawn remained on the ground, propped on one elbow and grinning again.

"Yeah," he shouted. "Now you're talking!"

Hoyle's hand felt as if it were broken, the pain causing him to feel like a fool. He had never hit anyone before, not even while playing sports in high school. The closest he came was when he grabbed onto and held another player during a brawl between his and another team. Even so, it took all his willpower to resist kicking Shawn and driving his yellow teeth down his throat.

Shawn stood up and spit, then wiped the grit from his elbows. "Man, fuck you." He spoke loud enough for Christine to hear. "You know why you're mine, baby, and always will be? Because your old man ain't willing to do shit about it." He poked Hoyle on the chest. "You've reached a fence and aren't willing to cross it. Can't I see the beauty of the night? Shit." He spat again, this time hawking blood on Hoyle's boots. "I see what might could bleed, old man. That's what I see." He then moved around to the driver's side of his car and opened the door. "Pack your bags, baby. I'll be back to pick you up in a day or so."

Hoyle was pelted with gravel when the car spun around and sped off. He watched it bounce down the drive and veer onto the road, the sound of its stereo lingering after it disappeared from sight. Back on the porch, where Christine stood with her back against the clapboard as if she wished to morph into the house, he stood staring at her, not knowing what to say or do to help her understand that their lives would soon return to normal, and that the ugliness of Shawn needn't touch them if they didn't want it to, and that they could keep it at arm's length. What he wanted to tell her was how dirty and tired he felt, as if the eruption of violence had spewed ash into the air that covered his face and hands that sapped his energy, and to point at his skin and say, "See? That's what comes from doing what I did. I should have stayed in the house and let him be and waited for the law to take care of him." But instead he mustered only, "It's okay. A deputy will be here in a few minutes. Then we can get back to doing what we were doing."

Christine seemed as if she hadn't heard him, and continued staring at the end of the drive, the expression on her face reminding Hoyle in a strange way that confused him of one he'd seen on his mother the day they brought his father to the hospital after the man's third and final heart attack, his mother staring at a door in the waiting area as if expecting her husband who'd looked after her for thirty-seven years to reappear.

Christine said almost nothing to the deputy who responded to their call, a big man bordering on fat whose eyes roamed around their house as if he were searching for stolen goods. Later, she ignored Hoyle when he bid her goodnight and stayed up late watching TV, an ashtray propped on her lap. Hoyle could hear the TV in his bedroom, the sound of it seeping through the floorboards and seeming to levitate his mattress, as if it might soon push him up and out the window into the night.

The next day Hoyle called Travis to find out if Shawn were in custody.

"No," he said, "he's gone to ground. I even personally checked his momma's place. But don't worry. He'll turn up pretty soon. He's smart, but not very bright, if you know what I mean. In a couple of days, we'll get him for something stupid like trying to drag race a deputy, just to brag about how fast he was going."

Hoyle was thinking about Christine and how nervous she now seemed, fidgeting all the time and playing with her hair. "He said he was coming back."

Travis said: "I hear you laid him out."

Hoyle felt too embarrassed to respond.

"Next time, don't let him get up," Travis said. "Do something. Hell, even sit on him to make sure until we get there."

Hoyle was revolted by the idea of again touching Shawn. He never mentioned to Diane that he'd punched the man, only that he'd been angered by him and that he feared what would happen when the man returned, as he surely would, and that he feared not being able to predict what might happen, and that anything was possible.

He said: "I feel like I'm trying to drive by looking into the rearview mirror. Does that make sense? Like I'm having to guess what's coming next by what I've just passed."

Diane was finishing fixing him a roast beef sandwich with thick slices of tomatoes and lettuce. Her kitchen smelled of exotic spices he couldn't name.

"This isn't fair, this whole thing. Look at you. You're tired all the time, agitated. You're not eating well." She served him the sandwich and poured him a glass of iced tea. "Wouldn't you like to go away somewhere? Maybe take a few weeks at the beach? Hilton Head or Figure Eight Island? We could rent a house, do nothing but sit on the beach all day. Swim, bike ride, maybe rent a boat. Eat like pigs. Maybe lay in bed 'til noon, making love, me resting and feeling secure in your strong arms. It'd be lovely."

Hoyle could picture the scene she described, could see them wearing shorts and walking hand-in-hand. But he shook his head, as if he were trying to shake off drunkenness. "I can't leave Christine. She's not ready for that, not now."

"Of course, of course. But we could take her with us. Some of those houses are like three stories. It'd be as if she were staying in an apartment all by herself. And she'd be away from all this nonsense and have time to think about her future, and maybe where she'd like to settle down."

The idea was like a carpenter bee burrowing a hole and making a nest in his brain. Maybe. She kept using the word maybe. He started to think, "Maybe I could." It sounded good. "But I have to work. And anyway I can't really afford anything like that."

"Oh my gosh, don't worry about money," Diane said. She perched on her knees on a stool and leaned her upper body on her elbows on the granite countertop so that Hoyle could see her cleavage. "Seriously. I've got plenty. More than I know what to do with."

Her suggestion to pay helped him knock loose the idea. Money did strange things to people, Hoyle knew, especially those who could never shed the notion that it always purchased something of value whenever it changed hands. For them, a gift was never a gift.

"Thank you. That's very kind," he said. "I'd love to go away with you someday. I really would, but can't right now. Not until after this mess is cleaned up. And not until Christine is in better shape."

He felt bad saying no to Diane, and worse when she shrank away from him, settling her weight on the backs of her calves. She wouldn't look at him, and stared instead at an imperfection in the granite she picked at with a fingernail.

She said: "I'm sorry. It's just that I miss you, Hoyle. Maybe you don't care. Or maybe you don't feel the same way. But I grow panicky when I think of losing you. You make me worry less about looking in mirrors."

Feeling guilty, and ashamed of what seemed his selfishness, he stood and embraced her, first stroking her hair, then kissing her neck. Holding hands, and moving upstairs into her bedroom where it smelled of cedar and lilacs, they removed their clothes, stepping out of and folding them as if they were in the dressing room of a department store and ready to try on a new pair of pants or skirt. He kissed her body, moving his hands across her breasts and stomach and thighs. He lay on top of her, watching how she closed her eyes and arched her neck. But he knew he was failing her, knew that he couldn't and wouldn't satisfy her in the way she most desired, and that he would leave with her looking after him and wouldn't look back for fear of seeing the disappointment in her eyes that he couldn't rectify, no matter how much he wanted or tried.

It was the same at home with Christine. Later, after returning from work, he found her in the living room, smoking cigarettes and watching a rerun of a sitcom. Judging from how the room smelled, and the amount of smoke hanging in the corners, he guessed she hadn't moved from the spot for much of the day.

He grabbed onto the banister and stepped upstairs, feeling as if at each next step he might slip through the boards into the basement. He felt insubstantial and as if he were no longer able to make his presence known or communicate his thoughts or desires, and that he would soon fade into oblivion. He lay awake long into the night, staring at the ceiling and dreading the passage of time.

When Shawn appeared the final time two nights later, and about two hours after the passage of a thunder storm which left behind a scent in the air of black dirt dug from deep in the ground, Hoyle felt a fear grow inside him that seemed to threaten to smother his heart, as if he were being filled with tar. He wasn't surprised by Shawn's arrival, knowing the man was here to see him as much as Christine. If not, why not come in the daytime when she was alone and he was at work? Seated on the porch, and watching the car bounce along the drive, he wanted to close his eyes and wish the man away to someplace else to never return. But Hoyle lifted himself from the chair and descended the stairs just as Christine emerged from the house, looking both scared and angry, like a hungry barn cat. The look caused Hoyle to pause for a half step before he said, "Call 9-1-1."

Christine didn't retreat and instead clung with both hands to the top of the stair railing.

Hoyle approached to just out of arm's reach to where Shawn stepped out of his car. His heart beating fast and high up in his chest, causing a sort of fluttering in his breathing, he said, "You might as well go home. You can say what you please, act like a fool, but you aren't going to get what you want."

Shawn stood with his hands on his hips and looked as if he were appraising a steer at a livestock auction. "Man, I always get what I want. Always."

Robert Boisvert

Hoyle heard Christine descend the stairs and run another few feet before stopping, as if she'd reached the end of a chain tethering her to the porch. "You get out of here, Shawn! I'm not going with you ever again! I mean it! You get out of here!"

Hoyle turned and stepped between her and Shawn, but not before he saw Shawn begin to smile. "Go inside the house, Christine. Go on. Get inside. Don't worry. No one's taking anyone anywhere."

Christine looked at him with a level of sadness that caused him to feel as if he'd swallowed a ball of ice. For a second, he couldn't be sure, he believed she wanted to say something to him, and that the first word would be "please." She then looked beyond him at Shawn before leaving and heading into the house, saying, "I'm telling you. You better leave."

Hoyle turned again to Shawn, seeing his smile had grown.

"See," Shawn said. "I told you I always get what I want."

Hoyle hated the other man. He hated his coarse attitude, and grimy clothes, and the hatred he spewed. He wanted to hit him again and cause him to cry out in pain. He imagined him falling to the ground, pleading for relief, one arm raised in supplication. He saw the blood and dirt and sweat streaking and speckling both their skins, felt the pain of what would be his cut knuckles and in his elbows and shoulders from the impact of the blows. And yet as the scene grew in detail and his scope broadened to include the house and barn and field and mountains, his hatred began to wane, as did his fear, and he felt again only pity for the other man and a desire to turn his back on him without saying a word.

He took a step forward. "Go home, Shawn."

Shawn's smile had turned to a smirk. "Or what? You going to hit me again?"

Hoyle felt tired. "There's nothing here for you. Christine's not going to go with you. She doesn't want to go. Do you understand that? You can make her, I suppose. But she won't stay because she doesn't need you anymore. As for me, I'm not sure what you want. Hatred. Fear. Blood. Your own blood. But whatever it is you aren't going to get it from me. You want to hit me? Okay. I might not like it. But I'm not going to hit you back. It's too sad. Really, I don't want to touch you. You want to shout and rave? Say mean and nasty things? Go ahead. I don't really care. But you aren't going to get a reaction from me."

He could see Shawn's smile begin to falter.

"Or is it that you want to talk?" Hoyle asked. "Is that it?"

Shawn was looking at him as if he were crazy. "What the fuck are you talking about?"

Hoyle heard Christine behind him reemerge onto the porch. "Is that what you want?" he asked. "To talk? Maybe go inside and drink a couple of beers? Talk about why we've arrived at where we are. I could, if you want. But the problem is I don't much like you. I pity you, really, and can't imagine you'd have anything worthwhile to say."

Shawn was staring at him as if he were imagining pulling back his skin and biting into his flesh. Hoyle braced himself, feeling anxious and a tingling sensation and almost magnetized pull in the areas around his jaw and nose and eyes and gut, areas where he expected to be hit, and he fought the urge to run.

But Shawn broke into a smile again, then began to chuckle, confusing Hoyle. "Man, you are so full of shit," he said. Shawn was looking now over Hoyle's shoulder at something behind him. He said: "Baby, I can't wait to shove that thing up your pussy," saying it as if he were savoring a sweet dessert.

Hoyle remembered Christine. He turned his head and saw and heard and felt in what seemed the same moment his daughter holding and pointing a pistol, the flash and explosion of several rounds, and a stinging pain in his upper arm.

Hoyle fell to the ground, clutching his arm, still wanting to shout, "No!" and forestall what had already occurred. His arm felt as it were being pressed onto a hot stove, the pain growing worse. He could feel blood between his fingers, slippery and sticky. Rolling to one side so that he could now feel dirt and grit mix with the blood, he saw Shawn on his back, his stomach arching upward, and fingers trying to claw into the ground; and to the other Christine looking from him to Shawn and seeming terrified, the pistol held halfway between the ground and horizon.

Hoyle climbed to his feet and approached his daughter. She seemed to have stopped breathing and stared at him as if she needed and craved advice on how to begin again. Using the hand covered in blood—his other arm seemed too heavy and bloated to lift—he reached for and took the pistol from her and tossed it aside.

Turning to Shawn, whose head lay beside the front left tire of his car, Hoyle approached and knelt beside him, knowing already the man couldn't be saved. He'd been hit in the neck, upper chest, and belly. Blood soaked his shirt and the ground beneath him, and oozed from his neck, giving off a stringent odor like rust. Hoyle also smelled feces as Shawn's body emptied its bowels. Shawn lay still now. Only his eyes and mouth moved as he saw Hoyle hovering over him. Hoyle couldn't understand what Shawn was trying to say. At first, the man seemed panicked, his eyes looking as large as boiled eggs. Then he seemed only sad, as tears welled in his eyes and as if he were realizing his life was nearly spent.

Hoyle held one of Shawn's hands, hoping to comfort him. Finally, he believed he understood the other man. Squeezing his hand, and scanning his eyes and face, he detected no vestige of the meanness or vileness or other traits of his personality he grew to hate and saw instead only despair and fear and regret and confusion and hope. It was as if the man were regressing in years and transforming into a child, scared of the dark and being abandoned. Hoyle recognized the child and sympathized with him, saw in how Shawn stared at him now the desire to be reassured and comforted and to be told, as if during a thunderstorm, the worst of it was over and clear skies would return.

When Shawn began to struggle for breath and his eyes grew wider and lost their focus, Hoyle gripped his hand in both of his and squeezed harder, as if to keep him from falling, but knew it would do no good and that the other man was no longer aware of his presence or ministrations. Shawn gulped from the air, trying to swallow mouthfuls of it, reminding Hoyle now of the animals he'd hunted and killed, in particular the deer which would run past the point of their hearts stopping and crash to the dirt where their mouths would expand and contract in this same manner like a machine running out of electricity.

Hoyle closed Shawn's eyes and waited a moment to offer a silent apology before standing and returning to Christine, who was crying.

"Is he dead?" she asked.

"Yes. He's dead."

Christine narrowed her eyes and appeared defiant. "Good, I'm glad. He deserved it for everything he did."

But Hoyle knew it was an act and wasn't surprised when she broke down and embraced him, burying her head in his shoulder.

"Oh my God, I'm so sorry," she sobbed.

Hoyle led her into the house and into the kitchen where he forced her to drink a double shot of scotch from a bottle he kept in a lower cabinet and hadn't touched in at least a year. She sat in a chair at the table and held the nearly empty glass between her thighs.

"I feel as if I'm trapped in a box," she said, staring at a point on the floor. "Everywhere I turn all I see is wall."

Hoyle was worried about her. Standing at the sink, and having taken off his shirt, he was examining the wound on his upper arm. Fortunately, the bullet had only grazed the muscle just above his elbow, taking off a chunk of flesh about a half inch square. The wound was still bleeding and still burned and had swollen the area around it. From the bathroom, and moving quickly, he retrieved a bottle of alcohol, gauze bandage, and a box of Bandaids. As he washed the wound in alcohol, the pain taking his breath away, he was thinking about Christine and when or even whether he should call the authorities. He didn't own any surgical tape and used the Bandaids to fasten the gauze into place. Glancing at Christine, and noting how she seemed to be slipping into a trance, he understood all at once he could never allow her to be locked up, and that prison would eliminate any remnant of sweetness within her and leave her bitter and hopeless.

He panicked a moment when he realized Christine might have called 9-1-1, remembering that he'd told her to call soon after Shawn arrived.

"Christine," he said, waking her from her daze. "Listen to me. Did you call 9-1-1? Earlier, did you call 9-1-1?"

Christine shook her head.

"Are you sure?"

Christine nodded her head.

Hoyle was relieved, but seeing now how she acted as if she were a child bolstered his determination to make sure she wasn't taken into custody.

Probably, considering Shawn's reputation, she'd be charged with something less than murder. He began to wonder if maybe she and he could claim self defense, tell the police that Shawn threatened to kill them, or came at them with a shotgun or knife, weapons Hoyle owned and could place in his hands. It didn't seem unreasonable, considering their earlier calls to 9-1-1 and the restraining order. He also wondered if maybe he could tell police that he killed Shawn, and leave Christine out of it entirely, tell police that he was wounded when he and Shawn struggled for the pistol, and that he shot him out of fear for his life.

But Hoyle knew he couldn't take the chance that Christine wouldn't be able to hold up under questioning and reveal the truth, and decided instead to hide Shawn's death. Taking her by the hand, and pulling her up out of the chair, he led her upstairs where he donned a new shirt and ran a bath and helped her remove her clothes. He felt no embarrassment as he viewed her naked body; only tenderness and a greater desire to protect her from harm as he lathered her arms and neck and back and armpits, feeling her soft skin and the layer of fat beneath it, and washed and rinsed her hair. Drying her hair, and wrapping her in a towel, he then led her into her bedroom where he gave her fresh underwear and a T-shirt and placed her into bed, pulling the covers up under her chin.

"I'm so sorry, Daddy," she said. "I'm so sorry."

Hoyle knelt beside the bed. "You be quiet now. No more of that. There's nothing to worry about. Daddy will take care of everything."

"Please forgive me."

He placed a kiss on her forehead and stroked her damp hair. "There's nothing to forgive. The sin is mine, baby. I know that now. Not yours. Now go to sleep. And when you wake up it will all be as if it never happened. I promise."

Hoyle tiptoed downstairs after turning off the light, and closing her door. Outside, he grabbed several strands of baling twine and a blue, plastic tarp from the barn which he spread on the ground next to Shawn's body. First checking to be sure the keys were in the ignition in Shawn's car, and grabbing the body by its arms, then its ankles, he heaved it onto the tarp and began rolling it and the tarp like a carpet. The pain in his arm increased as he moved, and he could feel the bandage coming loose, and blood matting his shirt, but he ignored them, as he did his revulsion as he felt the flesh shift and give way beneath the plastic, fighting the revulsion by thinking of the body as nothing more than the carcass of an animal, and nothing that spoke or thought or loved or hated.

After tying the tarp as tight as he could around the ankles, gut, and neck with the baling twine, and dragging it along the ground and into a pen in the barn which could be closed off from the horses, he hid it from sight by breaking open and covering it with several bales of hay. He would have preferred to tack two horses and haul the body now into the mountains where he might bury it or drop it into a gorge, but knew he didn't have time and would need to wait until tomorrow.

Making sure the pen was secure, and grabbing a rake and closing the barn doors, and after starting and moving Shawn's car, he unwound the hose attached to the side of the house and sprayed the area where Shawn's body had fallen. He used the rake to turn over the gravel and dirt, then sprayed the area again to be sure no blood remained. He then went into the kitchen and retrieved a bucket, dish soap, and rag and washed Shawn's car, just in case it too had been spattered by blood.

Next he gathered the pistol and shell casings and carried them into the kitchen where he removed his shirt and replaced his bandage, stuffing the old bandage and two bloody shirts into a plastic bag. Shoving the casings into a pant pocket, and tiptoeing upstairs, he replaced the gun in his room and grabbed another shirt. He waited a moment at the top of the stairs before heading back down to make sure he heard nothing coming from Christine's room, no crying or muttering.

The biggest problem, as he saw it, was going to be Shawn's car. He at first considered driving it along the field and path onto the logging road and pushing it into the second growth, since no one ever traveled back there but him. But he now suspected the low riding car might get hung up on any number of rocks and be unable to maneuver the rough terrain and incline. And what if he damaged the thing? What if he needed to tow it out of there and discovered he'd busted the transmission linkage or axle?

No, he knew he would need to drive the car someplace else, and hope he wasn't seen. Asheville would be ideal, considering Shawn lived and hung out there. But the walk back was too far to manage in the few hours he dared leave Christine alone, and he knew he couldn't take a bus or taxi or call a friend for a lift, since it would leave a trail of witnesses or seem too suspicious. Instead, he decided to drive the car into town and onto Route 251 where he would let the air out of one tire, making it seem as if Shawn had abandoned the car after getting a flat. To complete the illusion, and convince the authorities Shawn had needed to hitchhike a ride with another driver, all he needed to do first was open the trunk and empty the air from the spare.

But Hoyle grew worried as he started the car, and could feel his heart high up in his chest and in his eardrums where it seemed to expel small puffs of breath with each beat. The car smelled of spent cigarettes, body odor, and motor oil. He lowered the window, hoping to release the funk that seemed to want to strangle him. On the passenger seat were numerous CDs, packets of ketchup, a half empty bottle of Mountain Dew, and several plastic lighters. He drove just under the speed limit, despite his anxiety and growing desire to flee from the car. His greatest fear was what he might do to protect Christine if he were pulled over by a state trooper or deputy. It scared him when he thought about it for a moment before pushing it aside that he could not say for sure he would do X, as would be expected, and not Y or Z, or some other possibilities.

The ride to the intersection seemed to take hours instead of minutes. Each time a vehicle passed in the opposite direction he stared in the rearview mirror, praying he wouldn't see it slow and turn around. Fortunately, there wasn't much traffic on the highway. Even so, he hesitated pulling to the shoulder, not wanting to attract attention.

Steeling himself, and panicking now, he pulled to the side and jumped from the car barely before it stopped. Running around to the side opposite the road, and crouching down to hide from any drivers, he fumbled with the cap on the tire nozzle and began releasing the air, cursing that it took so long. He felt sweat beading at his hairline and armpits and the palms of his hands.

Afterwards, and after returning the cap to the nozzle, he began running through the second growth separating the highway from NC 22, feeling as if he were being pursued and about to be grabbed from behind. He reached the road out of breath and panting. His wound was throbbing, and he was drenched with sweat. The sweat loosened the bandage, causing the upper portion to sag so that he could feel blood trickling down his arm which he wiped occasionally onto his pants.

He began walking toward his house, thinking about the events that brought him here. He could feel the heat from the macadam cooling in the night, and could smell the warm tar and something dark and old like the soil around mushrooms seeping from the woods on each side of the road. Three times he ran into the woods and fell to the ground when headlights appeared on the horizon, waiting for the car to disappear from view, and wondering each time if the driver saw him. The last time, and before he returned to the road, he remembered the shell casings in his pocket and tossed them into the woods.

But what occupied him most was the question of whether or not he could have foreseen Shawn's death and prevented it. Hadn't Christine told him she needed more than love from him, that she needed him to protect her? He wondered if events might have turned out differently if he'd acted more forcefully when he first met Shawn, challenging or striking him. Maybe then Shawn might have learned a lesson and not decided to harass them. Or perhaps if he'd taken Christine away from the mountains and moved to Raleigh or the coast, maybe then Shawn might have lost track of and not followed them. Surely then she'd have been able to start a new life. Wasn't that what he should have done? Wasn't it his responsibility to do something?

Picturing Shawn's body wrapped in the blue tarp in his barn, and the sight of himself covered in sweat and grime and blood, he thought of himself as a criminal and failure. Imagining the black blood caked and dried on Shawn's neck, and the stiff limbs and the darkness of the skin on the lower portions of his body where the blood pooled and settled, he could perceive nothing good or worthwhile within himself, and grew certain that God had condemned him, believing more in God now than at any time in his life, feeling in an odd way that his guilt and sin had somehow empowered the heavens, and feeling even that Shawn's death and his failure had birthed a deity dedicated solely to his ruination.

Hoyle grew to fear the darkness of the woods, believing he could sense in the blackness angels hiding behind trees and under bushes poised to carry him to purgatory. For the first time in his life he suspected he did not know everything that dwelled and breathed upon the mountains, the suspicion causing him to grow queasy; and he hurried his pace, fearing now that he might be waylaid or prevented from making at least partial amends. He pictured Christine asleep in bed, then saw her waking, and believed now that allowing her to awake alone and scared and calling out in vain for him would be his greatest sin.

Hoyle became tired and dejected, at one point believing he was lost or had been transported to a place in which he did not recognize any landmark. When at last he saw his house and the lights glowing a dim yellow in the darkness, he began to trot and cursed his body for growing winded

Robert Boisvert

and not being able to maintain a speedier pace. Slowing as he neared the porch so as not to collapse, his feet falling flat on the gravel like flippers, he flexed the hand of his wounded arm which felt as if it were on fire, the arm itself feeling as if it were about to burst like a tick as he climbed the steps and opened the door, listening for any sound of distress in the silence.

Back upstairs, and opening the door to Christine's room, he was relieved to see her in the sliver of light from the hallway asleep on her side and seemingly at peace. He wanted only to bathe and fall into his own bed—his head felt now as if it were filled with hardening cement—but first he gathered a book of matches and the bag stuffed with bandages and shirts and carried them outside to an old and rusted grill near the side of the house that hadn't been used in years. Retrieving a can of gasoline from the barn, and careful to avoid looking in the direction of the pen where Shawn's body lay covered in hay, he undressed and placed all of his clothes on the grill and doused them in the gasoline.

The fire seemed unusually bright and hurt his eyes. Stepping away, and shielding his face from the brightness and heat, he felt a sense of relief and calmness, and breathed deeply. It was a strange sensation, as he felt at the same time a chill from the night air washing over his body, evaporating the sweat, making it seem as if he were invulnerable to the flames and already burned as black as soot. He waited until the fire died down before stirring it with a stick and pouring on more gas and lighting it again till only ashes remained.

Hoyle grabbed his boots and headed upstairs to shower. After lathering every portion of his body he could reach, and standing in the hot water for many minutes so that a thick fog of steam filled the bathroom, he dried himself and padded to his bedroom where he sat naked on the bed near the nightstand, examining his wound. It still hurt like hell, throbbing with each beat of his heart, but didn't look as bad as he expected. It had stopped bleeding for the most part and was covered now by a thin layer of what looked like mucus. Before climbing into bed, and after pulling on boxer shorts, Hoyle applied another bandage, this time fastening it with masking tape which he wrapped around his entire bicep, though not so tight it would cut off circulation. He lay on the bed, feeling as if he were being pressed between panes of glass. He pictured Shawn for a moment, and what he probably now looked like, then Christine looking helpless and scared. He remembered the feel of her arms around his neck, and hung tight to the image until falling into a deep sleep like dark water undisturbed by dreams.

PART THREE

He found Christine in bed beside him when he awoke the next morning. She was lying on her side with both hands beneath her head and staring at him, as if she'd been waiting a long time for him to open his eyes.

"Did I ever sleep with you like this when I was little?" she asked. "Were we ever happy like that? Or like we were supposed to be?"

Hoyle examined her face for a moment as if he were searching for any cracks or indication it might soon collapse, releasing a flood of emotions. He was relieved to see a sort of tired and distant resignation, suggesting she had accepted and given up fighting the reality of what happened the previous night. "Yes," he said. "Often."

"I'm sorry I don't remember it. Mostly I only remember wanting to remember it."

Hoyle pictured her as a toddler, chubby and laughing. "You were a happy child, and very loving."

"Really?"

"Yes."

"You know I really didn't want you to see me die like I said. Not really."

Hoyle nodded his head. "I know."

"I really wanted you to save me from dying. I wanted you to rescue me just at the last moment."

Hoyle felt a pang of regret and a warmth inside his chest, as if his heart had popped and were oozing honey. "I know," he said.

"Oh Daddy, what are we going to do?" She was looking at him as if she were ready to believe anything he said and follow any order. "I don't want to go to jail, but I need to know what's right."

"You're not going to jail. No one is. That's never going to happen." Hoyle hoped he sounded confident and didn't express any of the doubt he felt. "What happened last night wasn't your fault. Do you hear me? If it was anyone's fault, it was mine. I know now I should have done more to protect you, more to make sure you never ended up in that position and felt as if you were threatened and had no choice but to defend yourself."

She looked now as if she needed more from him, whether emotionally or physically he couldn't tell.

"You need to listen to me on this," he said, leaning forward and kissing her on the forehead. "It's going to be fine. Nothing bad will happen to you. I promise."

After rising and dressing in jeans and a T-shirt, and replacing his bandage, and making her breakfast and only coffee for himself, he phoned the brothers and told them to begin work without him. He saw Diane had called—she left a message saying she was "just checking in" and was wondering where he was and whether he had found another girlfriend, laughing unconvincingly. Hoyle was considering returning her call, but decided to wait until later, not certain he wouldn't somehow feel obliged to blurt out everything that happened and how he felt about events.

Christine didn't want to eat and sat at the table taking quick puffs from her cigarettes as if she were in a rush to finish the entire pack. Hoyle said nothing sitting across from her. His arm hurt, more of a dull ache than a sharp pain that hurt most when he tried to bend it at the elbow. Worse still was the black mood of an intense guilt and foreboding that seemed to be seeping into him like ink into cotton.

He gripped his mug of coffee with both hands. "Baby, you need to pack a bag."

Christine looked at him with something near horror. "I'm not going back to Momma's."

"No, baby. You need to go away. On your own. That's the only way I can protect you."

"But I don't want to go away. Please don't make me. I promise I'll be good."

"I know you will. And I don't want you to go either. I want you to stay here forever. But you need to leave just in case something goes wrong. It will be easier for me to convince people that you had nothing to do with what happened. Do you understand? If you're here, there's always the chance they can blame you and force you to accept responsibility. And I can't let that happen."

"But maybe if we go to them together and tell them we didn't have any choice, that we had to do it. Maybe they'll believe us and they'll let us alone."

"No, it's too late for that now, not with what I've done," he said. "And besides, it's time you made a new life for yourself. I see wonderful things in your future. I believe that with all my heart. I see love and children and happiness and contentment in your old age. You may not know it, but you've shown strength in these last few months. More strength than you know you possess. Certainly more strength than I possessed. You're ready now to strike out on your own and stand up without me or your mother or your friends or drugs to view tomorrow and every day after that with hope."

She was crying and shaking her head, but didn't object.

In the truck now with a small black bag between them and Christine leaning against the passenger's door, he drove first to his bank in Krodel. Christine had hesitated leaving the house, he guessed because she imagined she might see Shawn still lying in the driveway, and sat gazing out the window and sometimes at him as if she were a baby fascinated by twirling, shiny objects. Hoyle was trying to figure how much he might be able to withdraw. Altogether he possessed a little more than twelve thousand dollars: eight in a savings account, the rest in checking account. Much of the money in the checking account wasn't really his. Some of it he owed to the brothers for the last week's work. And some of it was Bob's, meant to pay for materials for the big house. But he figured he could get credit from the lumberyard for whatever he still needed and replace what he withdrew from the checking account with the remainder of what Bob owed him, and only hoped the man wouldn't delay payment. If he did, the hell with it, he figured. He'd deal with it later.

He asked the teller, a woman named Suzanne with long gray hair who waddled when she walked, even though she wasn't fat, how much he needed to keep in the accounts to keep them open.

"I hope you're not thinking of leaving us and taking your business elsewhere, Hoyle," she said. "We'd miss you."

Hoyle tried to think of a good excuse for taking all his money that wouldn't cause suspicion. "No, no. Just thinking I might buy me a new truck." He pointed a thumb over his shoulder. "Old one's giving me trouble."

"I know how that is," she said. "Half the time I head out in the morning not knowing if mine's going to start." She then told him neither account required a minimum balance and that they'd remain open for a while even if he had nothing in them.

He wrote a check for four thousand two hundred dollars and a withdrawal slip for eight thousand.

Suzanne looked at the papers as if she were confused by them. "You know we can print you up a cashier's check."

Hoyle was beginning to feel nervous and hoped it didn't show. One time he caught her glance at his bruised and swollen arm and was wishing now he'd worn a long sleeved shirt. "Thanks, but this guy, see, who's selling the truck, is one of those guys who prefers cash."

"But a cashier's check is as good as cash."

"Yeah, I know, but this guy, see, cash is fine. Really." He smiled at the woman, but was growing aggravated and wanted to yell at her to hurry up and mind her own damned business.

"Okay, but you know I have to tell the government. You know that, right?"

Hoyle felt a pang of terror like someone took a jab at his heart and were trying to cram it up his windpipe. "Why? What do you mean?"

"It's the law. Any time a customer withdraws more than ten thousand dollars in cash we need to fill out a currency transaction report."

Hoyle was angry now. He could feel the anger oozing down and hardening around his abdomen like molten lead. "But why? It's my money."

"Hoyle, it's no big deal. It's just a form." The woman seemed amused by his reaction, which fueled his anger.

"You think this is funny?" he asked. He was surprised by his desire to lash out at her, even to strike her.

The woman furrowed her brows. "What?"

"I don't think I should be hassled about wanting my own money."

The woman shook her head. Then she stared at him for a moment before turning towards a colleague.

"Just give me my money," he said, having decided he didn't like the woman and maybe never had, recalling instances in which she adopted a superior attitude. He didn't feel sorry for how he was acting, believing it was her own fault for treating him and probably others with disdain and disrespect.

The woman counted out and slid the stack of one hundred dollar bills towards him without looking him in the face. "I'm still going to have to fill out the form," she said.

Hoyle grabbed the bills and left the bank without responding, now feeling more disgusted than angry.

Back in the truck where Christine was looking like a dog worried its master might not return, Hoyle took three of the bills and handed the rest to her, telling her to stuff them in her pockets.

Christine stared at the money. "What's this for?"

"It's yours," he said, maneuvering the truck back onto the road. "It's for you to live on until you get a job."

"But this is too much. I don't want to take all your money," she said.

"Just do as I say, Christine. Don't argue with me. Put the money in your pockets. Your front pockets so no one can get at it. And don't go flashing it around. If you need some of it, go into a bathroom or someplace private and take out one bill at a time. Don't let anyone see you got this big wad of money. The same as when you get to where you're going. Hide it good. It's nobody's business but your own."

Christine did as she was told, and pushed the bills into her front pockets.

Hoyle was staring at the road and trying not to think about the future. Maybe it was because of the teller or because of Christine's sad expression, but he was filled now with a greater sense of foreboding, more intense than before, having for some reason pictured police gathered around Shawn's car and rooting around his property. Feeling as if something terrible were about to happen, and as if he couldn't avoid it, he drove with both hands tight on the wheel, as if he expected the pavement to crumble and fall away into nothing beneath them.

They arrived at the Greyhound bus station in Asheville about a half hour later. Hoyle used his good hand to carry her bag and held one of hers with the other, leading her into the waiting area. It hurt, the way she squeezed his hand, but Hoyle didn't flinch or pull away. He sat her in an orange colored plastic chair bolted to the floor and set the bag on her lap. The station smelled like spent cigarettes, musty cardboard, and pine scented cleanser. The few other passengers eyed them for a few moments before refocusing on their newspapers or the various televisions hanging from the ceiling.

Hoyle stepped to the counter and bought a one way ticket to Raleigh using part of the three hundred dollars he'd taken from the stack he'd given to Christine. He then called information for the number to Amtrak and dialed it to find out when the next train left for someplace north.

"Listen," he said, sitting beside her and handing her the ticket. "Pay attention now. This is to Raleigh. When you get there, get in a cab and tell the driver to take you to the nearest Marriot or Sheraton or someplace like that. Nothing cheap. You hear me? Pay whatever they want, but make sure it's nice and in a safe neighborhood. Then tomorrow morning take another cab to the train station. There's a train leaving at 8:54 to Washington, DC. From there it's your decision. You can go to New York, Boston, Chicago, California. Wherever you want. Just pick a place you've always wanted to go and can see yourself living."

Christine was already shaking her head and crying. "I don't want to go. I'm scared. I want to stay here with you."

"Listen to me. Now stop that. It's okay to be scared. But if you stay here you'll never live the life you want. It will always be the same. You'll never get anywhere beyond where you are now."

"I'm sorry. I'm so sorry."

"I told you, don't say that. Don't say that ever again." Hoyle glanced around to be sure no one could hear them. "What happened was my fault. Not yours. I killed that boy. Me. I did it. Just as surely as if I pulled the trigger myself. I killed him by what I didn't do for all those many years. By not keeping you close and protecting you. I did it. Do you understand? Tell me you understand."

Christine continued shaking her head.

"Say it. Say you understand," he said.

"I understand."

"I will always protect you. You will never, ever again have to worry about what happened. From this moment on, right now, you need to believe with all your heart that what happened wasn't your fault. You need to believe your father when he says that you are in no way guilty of what happened, that only I am and I alone. Do you hear me?"

"Yes."

"Now I want you to promise me you'll stay away, even if you're scared and homesick. Just for a year or so. Set yourself a time limit, and that will help you get over your fear. Then pretty soon you'll find that you're not scared any more, and maybe you'll like where you are. And don't tell anybody where you are. Not your mother, no one. Just in case."

"Just in case of what? What's going to happen?" She recoiled to look at him full in the face.

"Nothing's going to happen. Stop it. I mean just in case they give your number or address to some of your old friends," he lied. "You need to start fresh, find other friends. You don't need them interfering with your new life and trying to cause trouble."

Edging closer, and wincing as he lifted it, he placed his wounded arm around her shoulder, cradling her head. "Settle down now. I promise you it will be different than it was," he said. "You'll be safe. You'll see. You'll never have to worry again. Not ever."

More people began entering the station. Hoyle followed with his eyes a short, fat, pregnant young woman with long black hair hauling a cheap suitcase and followed by a dirty boy about three years old sucking his thumb, envying both the boy and the mother. When it was announced that the bus would depart in ten minutes, and passengers gathered around it and handed their bags to the driver, Christine wiped her eyes and looked at him with a sort of eagerness that both pleased and saddened him. He led her to the bus, saying it was time to go.

"I'll miss you," she said.

Hoyle smiled, knowing she wouldn't, not in the same way he would miss her. He hated this moment and the realization that the girl he was kissing goodbye would never return.

"I'll miss you too," he said, and watched her board the bus and take a seat by a window in the rear. Hoyle stayed until the bus left, never taking his eyes off her as she smiled one moment, and blinked away tears the next. When the bus roared away, filling the area with diesel fumes, he felt a relief and a surge of anxiety, one after another, as he waved and wanted to run forward and push the bus and speed it towards its destination.

Now in his truck and heading back home, he began to think about how to get rid of Shawn's body. He didn't want to tackle the chore. The idea of touching the body and smelling its foulness caused him to shudder and feel queasy. But he knew the job couldn't be avoided no matter how much he wanted, and tried to decide how best to go about doing it. Should he bury it in the field, that way making sure he could always keep an eye on it, so to speak, and no wayward hunter might come across the bones? Or should he cart it into the mountains, as he first envisioned, thereby doing away with the fear that the authorities might notice a freshly dug grave, or would always be able to pin the death on him or Christine, since the body was buried on his property? Even if some hunter did find the bones, couldn't he argue that anyone might have dumped the body on the mountains?

Then he remembered a small cave on the northern side of the second Skull he'd discovered as a child. He remembered being fascinated by its coolness and musky smell, imagining a bear or coyotes once lived there, and being disappointed he didn't find the bones of their small prey. It would be a tight squeeze—the thing probably wasn't really much more than a nook or indentation in the rock—and wouldn't be easy to get to, since the terrain in the area slanted at a near thirty-five degree angle. But if he could somehow wedge the body far enough inside and seal the opening with rocks large enough to keep any animals from getting to it, he doubted anyone would ever discover what happened to Shawn.

He began thinking about the equipment he would need. Rope to lower the body. A pick ax to widen the cave, if needed. A pry bar and sledgehammer to move and bust nearby boulders and rocks for the opening. The idea that he might also need the sledgehammer to break Shawn's bones in case his legs or arms needed to be bent further than was natural caused him to want to vomit. But as he was nearing his house and thinking how best to tie the body and tools to one of the horses, and which horse might carry them best without spooking, he saw Diane's car in his driveway and swore out loud, wondering if he should drive past and return only after he was certain she'd gone. He slowed the truck and craned forward in his seat to see if he could catch sight of her, and turned only at the last moment after imagining her somehow stumbling across the body.

He found Diane sitting on the steps of the porch and looking as if she'd been caught doing something wrong. Her eyes seemed as round and fleshy as plums.

"I'm sorry for just showing up like this," she said. "Don't be mad. But I didn't want to risk calling again and getting your voicemail. I feel like I'm being locked in a file cabinet when I talk to that recorded voice."

Hoyle looked toward the barn to be sure everything was the same as he left it, then sat beside her. Diane didn't turn towards him and stared straight ahead at the road, looking like she meant to fight him if he tried to move her, the way she arched her back and held so tightly to the bottom lip of the stair her knuckles were white.

"I wish you'd just tell me," she said. "I can't take it anymore. I wish you'd just tell me that you don't want to see me anymore. I'd understand. Really I will. But I don't want to feel this anxiety anymore. I'd rather feel heartache or pain, anything but this. I'd rather know for certain things between us are over and not wonder all the time when they're going to end."

Hoyle felt ashamed listening to her, knowing he had abandoned her over these last few days. He also felt a surge of anxiety as it occurred to him that he might lose her forever and not be able to salvage their relationship because of the secret that of necessity must remain between them. Looking at her, and wanting to pry her hands from the stair and embrace her, he craved to rest his head on her breasts and unburden himself of the ugliness of the situation and the chore that lay ahead of him, and to even solicit her advice and help.

"I'm sorry," he said, feeling now drunk with exhaustion and as if he might collapse if he tried to stand. "I've been busy with Christine. We've been trying to work things out between us. And I think we have. But she's gone now. Both of us realized she wouldn't be able to get her life straight hanging around here."

Diane stared at him now as if she suspected he were pulling a prank. "Really?"

Hoyle nodded his head. "I just got back from Asheville putting her on the bus."

"Where's she going?"

"To the train station in Raleigh first. Then to DC. After that, I'm not really sure. I told her to pick a place she could imagine herself living."

Diane unbent her back and relaxed her grip on the stair. "So this isn't just a vacation? It's a permanent thing?"

Hoyle remembered the sight of his daughter smiling and crying on the bus. "I guess. Pretty much, yeah."

Diane looked again towards the road. "So what about us? Is there any hope?"

Hoyle closed his eyes, not knowing how to respond. He felt bewitched and didn't want to think any longer about Diane and their future and the fact that she felt more passion for him and whether his emotions would ever change or this odd need for her that confused and comforted him in how it promised contentment and moments of happiness without deep love, or about Christine and her prospects or Shawn's killing or his body. He pictured riding alone into the mountains towards the cave and how relieved he would feel to place himself inside it like a bear and hibernate until the spring.

"Do you want me to go?" she asked.

The question prompted an immediate inner alarm. Of course she needed to go. Of course she couldn't stay and risk involvement in murder. He told himself he needed to physically remove her, to drag her to her car if necessary and to shout and holler at her, say anything to make sure she left. But he stayed where he was beside her, feeling too exhausted to move or speak, and telling himself while beating back his shame that he would allow her to remain for a only a little while, just until he caught his breath, and wouldn't in any way reveal what had happened between him, Christine, and Shawn.

He shook his head without opening his eyes.

"I'll make you happy," she said. "I promise. You'll see. We'll make a happy life together just like in a fairy tale."

She stood and took him by the hand, pulling him up the stairs. "Oh my God, what happened to your arm?"

Hoyle looked at it, surprised by its mottled color and swollenness. "Nothing. An accident with a power tool."

She pulled up the sleeve of his T-shirt to look at the bandage. "Are you sure it's not infected? Did you go to a doctor?"

Hoyle pulled his arm away. "It's nothing. Really, I'm fine."

He suspected from the look in her eyes that she didn't believe him, and felt hurt that he was withholding a secret from her, but he didn't care and allowed himself to be led into the house and up the stairs into his bedroom where she laid him on the bed and took off his boots and socks. Retrieving a wet washcloth from the bathroom, and after removing the bandage, she washed his arm, wiping off any dried blood from his skin, and left it uncovered, saying it needed to breathe. She then lay beside him and rested her head on his chest, saying, "You close your eyes now," as if she somehow knew how exhausted he was by the events of the previous night and that morning.

He didn't at first know how long he slept, if at all, seeing in his mind a static and constant image of Christine on the bus, seeming forlorn and forsaken and not at all eager as he then imagined; but when he sat up he noticed the light in the room had dimmed and the air seemed cooler and he saw Diane folding clothes from a laundry basket and placing them in his bureau. She was gazing at him and smiling.

"Hello sleepy head," she said. "Feeling better?"

Hoyle felt depressed and sluggish, as if he were in the last stage of the flu, and swung his legs over the side of the bed to put on his socks and boots. "What time is it?"

"Nearly five," she said. "Dinner's almost ready. I found some hamburger in the freezer. I hope you don't mind I used it for spaghetti sauce. Or we can go out if you want."

Hoyle was angry with himself for delaying what needed to be done on the mountain and allowing Diane to stay. You're crazy, he told himself. Stupid. It's weakness and selfishness, nothing more. But he knew it was too late in the day to attempt hauling the body to the cave. Even if he could somehow get rid of Diane, and start out within the hour, he wouldn't arrive until sunset and would be forced to try to lower the body and seal it inside in the dark. His arm was throbbing again and he had difficulty tying his boots.

"Where are you going?" she asked, pushing a shirt into a drawer. "You okay?"

Hoyle turned at the door. "I need to feed the horses."

Diane was looking at him as if she were worried by or trying to figure out his mood. "Maybe we should bandage your arm again to make sure nothing gets in it."

Hoyle tried to smile. "I'll be careful. We'll do it later."

Outside, where the air smelled like cool water and green grass and manure from the field carried on a breeze, Hoyle felt what seemed like an almost repulsive force emanating from the barn like a magnetic field pushing against him as he approached it, moving tentatively, almost tiptoeing. His heart began to race, causing his arm to pulsate with pain, and bile rose in his throat as he entered the structure, expecting to smell putrefaction or to see liquid leaking from beneath the hay and pooled in the aisle. Skittering now past the pen and towards the feed room, he scooped grain into three buckets, not caring how much spilled on the floor and whether it would attract rats and left the barn by the back entrance, feeling right away a sort of reprieve from doom so that when he dropped the buckets on the ground for the horses trotting towards him and returned to the house he felt relieved to see Diane in the kitchen stirring a pot of sauce and was glad he had not insisted she leave.

The kitchen smelled of oregano and fried meat. He said little during dinner, and barely listened to Diane talking about her son visiting the next weekend and how she hoped to introduce the two of them. Hoyle felt tired again and was relieved when they moved to the living room where she bandaged his arm and they watched television and felt a greater relief as the sun set and darkness seemed to settle on the house like a quilt, as if they were hidden now from view. He felt comfortable and secure with her in his arms, and more so upstairs in bed, feeling the warmth and substance of her body and smelling her hair and the powdery scent of her skin, despite the foreboding and a nagging guilt for his weakness and selfishness and having dodged the chore of disposing of Shawn's body. He fell asleep to the sound of Diane's breathing, her fingers caressing his chest.

When he awoke in the morning with the sunlight spread over the bed and floor like beurre blanc, and smelled on the breeze through the window fresh dirt, he panicked for a moment, certain Diane had wandered into the barn and discovered the body. He could hear her downstairs in the kitchen, working with pans and plates and running water. He knew, of course, she hadn't, realized she would have woken him if she had, but he couldn't shake the suspicion as he shuffled into the bathroom, then dressed and pulled on his boots, that she'd discovered some portion of the truth and his guilt.

The suspicion dissipated when he saw her smiling at him and scooping scrambled eggs onto a plate, and looking vulnerable and lovely without her makeup, as if she'd just scrubbed her face, and was replaced by a shame greater than that he felt the previous night, an emotion that seemed to soak him and stream from his skin and slide down his torso and legs like sweat. Watching her, and seeing how she seemed to glide across the floor as if on skates, he wanted to hoist her in his arms and carry her to her car, and offer an apology and kiss and tell her he didn't deserve her kindness.

"I thought you'd like something hearty before heading to work," she said. "My mother always called these Irish eggs. Scrambled eggs with cheese. I'm not sure why, but they're good."

The smell of the food made him queasy, but he forced himself to eat, knowing he would need his strength for the job ahead of him. He also didn't want to disappoint Diane or cause her any further concern.

"Your arm looks better," she said. "How does it feel?"

Hoyle lifted and flexed it. "Good. Still a little stiff." He was already thinking about the body and the location of each of the tools he would need and how to tie them to the horses, and how much food he should eat before he could lie and tell Diane he needed to leave for work. He only hoped Diane wouldn't suggest she stay at his house to clean or cook for him or some fool thing and would want to return to her own home. He was trying to think of an excuse for why she shouldn't and one for if she asked to see him at lunch when he was startled by a knock at the front door.

Diane looked at him as if she learned he'd betrayed her. It occurred to him she probably believed Christine had returned. Hoyle stood and walked to the door, surprised to find Travis, standing with the heels of his hands resting on his holster.

Hoyle opened the screen door and stepped outside, trying not to panic. He was alarmed how the sight of the man in his uniform and the patrol car in his driveway prompted this odd urge to vomit the truth and tell him every detail of what happened.

"Hey Hoyle," Travis said. "How you doing?"

Right away Hoyle knew he was in trouble. He could see it in his friend's eyes and how they flitted like flies, taking in his own eyes, his arm, and Diane now standing in the doorway, and could hear it in his voice in how it seemed a portion of a chorus with each member singing out the same question but with different intentions, some friendly, some sinister. Pushing his hands into his pockets, and stepping off the porch into the sunlight so as to move out of earshot of Diane, he was surprised by how relieved and strengthened he felt by the realization, as if it were a wall he might leverage his weight against and push off of. Travis followed him onto the drive.

"Doing well. What can I do for you?" he asked.

Travis stared at Hoyle for a few moments, causing Hoyle to wonder if he'd said something wrong, or if the other man had spotted something incriminating. "Well, I'll tell you. I was wondering when's the last time you saw Shawn."

Both men turned at the sound of Diane stepping out onto the porch. Hoyle felt sorry for her, seeing the worry and timidity on her face and how she latched onto the stair railing as if it were a lifeline.

"How you doing, miss?" Travis asked, tipping his hat.

Hoyle said: "I don't know. A while back. I can't remember exactly."

"How long's a while?" Travis was talking louder now, as if for Diane's benefit.

"A few weeks, I guess. Right around the last time I called you."

Travis nodded his head. He was looking down at the ground as he rolled a pebble beneath the toe of a shoe. "So not recently?"

"You mean since then? No." Hoyle resisted the urge to ask why, not wanting to feed the man's suspicion.

"By the way, what happened to your arm?"

Hoyle glanced at his bicep. "Just an accident. Nothing, really."

"Really? Because it looks pretty nasty. What happened?"

Hoyle was flustered by the question and hoped he wasn't blushing. "A pneumatic hammer misfired on me. Took out a chunk of flesh."

Travis tilted his head and inched it forward. "I'm trying to picture it," he said. "Seems like an odd angle to get hit."

Hoyle said nothing.

"Anyway," Travis continued, "reason I'm asking about Shawn is because we found his car abandoned on 251 and since it's just up the road from here and this ain't his usual haunt I was wondering if he was heading from your house."

Hoyle shook his head. "No, not from here."

"Christine around? Maybe we should ask her."

Hoyle stiffened his back, as if expecting to be shoved. He had trouble meeting Travis's eyes, and resisted looking away.

"She's not here, is she?" Travis asked. "Where is she, Hoyle?"

Hoyle said nothing.

"You're not going to tell me? Is it a secret?"

"She's gone away," Hoyle said. "We thought it was time for a new start. I put her on the bus yesterday."

"Uh huh." Travis nodded his head. "Gone away. With twelve thousand dollars?"

Hoyle felt isolated suddenly and vulnerable, as if he were standing naked in a snow storm. He turned to Diane for reassurance, but felt further isolated when he saw only fear and confusion on her face.

"Hoyle, what the hell is going on?" Travis asked.

Hoyle tried smiling. "What do you mean? Nothing."

"Seriously. Come on. Look at me, Hoyle. What's going on?"

"Nothing's going on. I don't know what you mean."

"You don't know what I mean?"

"No, I don't. I'm having breakfast, and you knock on the door, and you ask me if I've seen Shawn, and I say no, and then you ask me what the hell is going on. Like I'm supposed to know something. What do you want me to say?"

Travis stared again at Hoyle, then nodded his head, as if he'd decided something. "So that's it? That's all you got to say to me? To me? Your friend? That's all you got?"

Hoyle could feel the sweat squeezing through his skin, the feeling like pins and needles in his armpits. "About what?"

"About what," Travis repeated, clearly angry. "Okay. That's the way you want it. How about this? How about the fact that I find Shawn's car in a place it has no right being, except if he came to visit you or Christine? Or the fact that it's made to look like he got a flat tire, except there's nothing wrong with the tire as far as I or anyone else can tell. Or that he left his keys in the ignition, which makes no friggen sense at all. I mean, if he was walking to a gas station or got picked up by a friend, why the hell wouldn't he take his keys?" He paused a moment. "Any idea?"

Hoyle stared at Travis, trying his best to hate him.

"I didn't think so," Travis said. "Or how about the fact that one of his idiot friends said he was specifically coming here two nights ago? Said he was going to have some fun and set you straight. Or the fact that his car looks like it was washed by a monkey, with these big streaks of dirt and missed spots, making me think someone did it in a hurry. You know, as if they were trying to hide something. Like something bad they didn't want anyone else to see. You know?"

Travis shook his head, then gazed past Hoyle's right shoulder up at the sky, as if he were partly embarrassed by what he was saying. "Or how about the fact I'm having coffee the other day? I'm over at Mary's, and Bill Lentz, the manager of the bank, comes over and says, 'What's with Hoyle?' And I say, 'What?' And he says, 'He nearly bit Suzanne's head off and withdrew pretty much every penny he has. In cash.' Then I do a little more checking and, sure enough, a man and a woman fitting your and Christine's description were at a bus station in Asheville yesterday morning. So I come here and I see your arm all purple and yellow that sure as shit wasn't caused by any hammer, and you're acting like you don't know me. Like I'm some stupid cracker you can shrug off with your lame answers. 'What?

What are you talking about? About what?' I mean, Hoyle, really. The boy was the worst type of bastard. I'll give you that. Maybe it was an accident. Maybe it couldn't be helped. Or maybe Christine just couldn't take it anymore. Hell, I wouldn't blame her. But what am I supposed to think? You tell me. What am I supposed to think is going on?"

Hoyle now felt as if he'd grown detached from his body and were watching the scene between the two of them from above, like those stories of people with near death experiences. Looking at Travis, and seeing the determination and doubt and compassion in his eyes, he hated the fact that he felt a need to hate his friend, especially when hearing him say Christine's name. Hoyle stared at him, accepting the realization he would not hesitate swinging at and hurting him, and that he wouldn't care. Not at first. He wanted to explain the situation to him, and why he did what he did, and why it was now the way it was and couldn't be changed, and tried to think of anything to say, but instead shrugged his shoulders.

Travis set his jaw and pursed his lips, as if he too had decided to hate his friend. "I think I'm going to take a look around now, Hoyle."

Hoyle stepped forward and shook his head. "No, Travis. Not without a warrant."

Travis arched his back. He stared at Hoyle. "You grow some balls, Hoyle? Is that what happened? You going to stop me?"

Hoyle clenched his fists, surprised by how tall and strong he felt. He liked the feeling. "I think maybe it's time you were leaving."

Travis narrowed his eyes, looking as if he might relish swinging at Hoyle. Then he took a deep breath and held it a moment before exhaling. "I'll be right up there," he said, pointing to the road. "I'm calling it in and will have the warrant in about an hour. Don't try running, Hoyle. I wouldn't like that. Understand?"

Hoyle said, "I understand," but knew Travis had already stopped listening. He waited until the man backed his car up the drive and parked near the entrance on the road before turning to Diane. She was staring at him with a pained expression and disbelief that reminded him of Shawn the moment after he'd been shot. He knew what he had to do, having seen it in his mind the moment Travis said, "Maybe Christine just couldn't take it anymore," accepting it with equanimity, as if he'd known all along it needed doing so that he felt a fool now for trying anything else.

"You need to leave," he said. "You can't be a part of this."

Diane was shaking her head, as if she was unwilling to listen to him. "She's made her choices. You can't live her life for her. She can't ask you to pay for her mistakes. This is our time now."

Hoyle climbed the steps and pried her hands from the railing. "Please, Diane. I need you to do as I say."

"I know it was her. And so does that deputy. Whatever it was that happened, he and others will know it was her fault. Don't you see? It doesn't matter what you do. They're going to get her anyway."

Hoyle pulled her down the stairs.

"Let's go away," she said, digging in her heels and turning him around so that they stood now face-to-face. "Right now, let's go away. I know this beautiful spot near Lake Tahoe where we can ride horses into the mountains just like here. Then we can go to Palm Beach or Martha's Vineyard while we wait for you to get a passport. Afterwards, we can take a train to every city in Spain. Or we can drive in the fall in the Pyrenees just as the air is beginning to turn cold and the inns are preparing to close for the winter. We can live in Paris or Vienna or St. Petersburg. We can live the lives we were supposed to live. Finally, we can live for ourselves and no longer need to suffer for the sake of others. It will be like when we were young and unfettered and hadn't yet made the mistakes that would shackle us for years, only better because we won't always be in a rush and can savor and appreciate whatever it is we come across. We'll be free and happy and no longer haunted by our pasts. I've seen it, Hoyle, and it's beautiful. I swear to you I've seen it as clearly as I see you now, you and I laughing and making love and holding hands and living life as if we expected the next day to be sweeter than the last, as it should be lived. Don't think about it. Don't ruin it by mulling it over. There's always a reason not to do something. Just come away with me. Get in the car and come away with me now."

Hoyle could picture the scenes she described, could see the cobblestone streets and ancient buildings. He could see himself tasting spicy dishes containing rice and olives and unusual meats and fish served by waiters in long aprons and bow ties. He imagined looking across the table at her one night and seeing how her face seemed to glow in the candlelight, and maybe even falling in love and saying to her, "Thank you," and, "You were right, this is beautiful," and, "You're beautiful," and, "I love you." Looking at her now, looking pale in the sunlight outside his house, he was struck by the thought that she seemed then the most beautiful woman in the world. He squeezed her hand, feeling the sweat on her palm, and imagined himself saying, "Yes, alright. You go ahead and get ready. Let me finish here with Travis. That can't be avoided. Then I'll meet you at your house," and hoping she didn't see through the lie.

He said: "You know I can't"

Diane would no longer look at him. "You're so stupid," she said. "My friends think I'm a fool for falling in love with you, a carpenter from nowhere. They think it's only because you were kind to me and weren't a challenge and because I'm on the rebound from a bad relationship. But they don't understand that love should be cherished whenever it's found and shouldn't be questioned because it's so rare. And neither do you. I know you don't love me, but I know you could if you would let go of your guilt and sense of duty and let yourself. And I know you'll miss me."

She moved to her car and dug in a pant pocket for her keys. "You'll regret this," she said. "You'll see."

Hoyle suspected a part of what she said was right. He wanted to explain to her how beautiful he believed her to be, and how much he enjoyed her company and reveal some measure of his affection, but was already looking beyond her at Travis in his patrol car. Having seen the movement of his eyes, and after climbing into her car and slamming the door, Diane sped away so that the car fishtailed along the drive and kicked up a cloud of dust.

Hoyle wasted no time watching her turn onto the road. Moving inside and upstairs to his bedroom, and seeing every step of what he needed to do as if they were scenes in a movie, he grabbed his father's Winchester Model 70 and two boxes of cartridges, which he stuffed into a game bag he slung around his neck. He thought about taking the handgun too, considering he hadn't fired the rifle in several years, but decided he wouldn't need it, that it would probably only get in the way, and headed downstairs to the kitchen where he grabbed two lighters, his best folding knife, a canteen, some sheets of paper, a pen, and an envelope before opening the side door and jogging to the barn.

Setting the rifle against the side of the barn hidden from view from the road, where he also dropped the game bag, he retrieved a bucket of grain and two lead lines from inside the barn using the rear entrance and spread the grain on the ground in three piles for the horses already trotting towards him. As usual, the two bay geldings chased away the gray, but Hoyle captured the gray and attached a lead line to its halter to a ring bolt on the side of the barn. He did the same with the larger of the two bays, pulling it away from the gray and attaching it to a second ring bolt. When the other bay continued harassing the gray, and lowered its head and nipped it on the neck, causing the gray to pull on the lead and try to flee, Hoyle grew furious and swung at the bay, hitting it on the mouth and hollered and kicked at it, chasing it away. "You stupid son of a bitch! Leave him alone," he shouted, and stared at the thing standing and trembling about twenty feet distance to be sure it didn't cause any further trouble before heading back inside the barn and hauling out two saddles, bridles, pads, cinches, and rope.

He first tacked the gray, then the bay, cinching the saddles tighter than normal to try to keep anything from slipping on the ride. Next he hauled Shawn's body from the pen, dragging the blue tarp across the ground. The thing did not stink as much as he expected—only occasionally would he catch a whiff of the sweetness of rotting meat—but it had swollen from when he last saw it, like a sausage first thrown in a frying pan. He figured it was probably because of trapped gas in Shawn's stomach, and doubted he would be able to bend the body over the bay's back if it remained. Fearing he was running out of time, and despite his disgust, he grabbed a leather awl from the barn and plunged it into what he calculated was the body's abdomen. Holding his breath, and extracting and tossing aside the awl, he then pushed with all his weight on the body, releasing the gas. The foulness of the gas which he somehow smelled despite not breathing and the bubbly sound it made caused him to retch and instinctively scramble backwards, as if he were in danger of being burned. The horses too tried to bolt and pulled on the leads and calmed only when he grabbed their halters and spoke softly to them and petted their necks.

Grabbing the tarp, after having first placed more grain in front of the horses to keep them preoccupied, and tossing the half empty bucket towards the other bay, he slung the body over the back of the bay and began securing it in place with the rope. Because of rigor mortis, and despite the release of the gas, Hoyle still had difficulty bending the body which seemed as tough as dried and cracked leather, but he eventually fastened it by tying one end of the rope around the neck, looping it around the saddle horn, winding it around the ankles, slipping it through the noose around the neck, and hauling with all his might, the exertion causing his wounded arm to feel as if it were being stabbed. He finished the job by wrapping the rope around the body's neck and ankles and the barrel of the horse several more times, hoping it wouldn't chafe the bay and prompt it to kick out.

Now satisfied, and after having bridled the gray and tied the reins to the lead line still attached to the barn to keep it from spooking when he began shooting, Hoyle picked up the Model 70, loaded it with three cartridges, and stepped to the edge of the barn to where he could see through the trees Travis's car on the road. His arm hurt like hell again and trembled when he practiced raising the barrel. Steadying himself by leaning against the corner of the barn, and having chambered one round, he took aim, breathed deeply through his nose, smelling the oil on the wood, held his breath, and squeezed the trigger. The report was louder than he remembered and caught him unawares, but he quickly ejected the casing, chambered another round, took aim again, and fired.

He secured the rifle by wedging it underneath several loops of the rope around the bay. Slinging the game bag around his neck, and untying the gray, and taking hold of the bay's lead line, he mounted the gray and set off across the field towards the mountains, taking a route that would bring him in plain view of anyone standing on the road. He couldn't be positive, but was fairly certain he hit the car at least once, probably twice, either in a tire or the engine block. His hope that Travis had jumped from the car and was watching him was satisfied when he heard a shot behind him sounding like a firecracker, Hoyle guessing the man made the futile gesture of firing his pistol at this distance either out of anger or as a warning that he'd soon be following.

Hoyle moved at a slow pace, giving the gray its head, not wanting to upset the load on the back of the bay, and knowing it would take a couple of hours for the sheriff's office to cart in enough men and ATVs to track him. Entering the path, and glad that the breeze was blowing towards him and away from the stench of the body, he felt a black mood take hold of him as he relaxed and no longer worried about rushing from his homestead, and images of Christine and Diane and Shawn and what lay ahead crowded his mind. The mood grew in extant as he entered the shade of the woods on the logging road where the air felt thick like syrup on his lips and nostrils until the mood seemed then an external force, belittling and berating him. He hunched his shoulders and lowered his head, as if against a driving rain, feeling as if he could hear the trees and mice and toads and other small animals whispering about him and sniggering.

He heard his father. "I'm right here, boy. Hush up now." Hoyle remembered his father backtracking through the woods to where he knelt in the snow, waiting for his return. The father had left the small boy for many minutes to follow a set of tracks that branched off from another set to see if perhaps they belonged to a huge buck they'd spotted once about three weeks earlier but had never been able to catch up to close enough for a shot. At first, Hoyle felt invigorated by his solitude. He felt a tenseness in his limbs, as if they were wound to spring him forward, and pictured himself as a bobcat lying in wait to leap upon a rabbit. Then he heard the creaking of the trees, and the wind rattling the upper and frozen branches, the sounds seeming to fall like dead beetles on the snow and rime covered brown leaves and pine needs layering the ground, and he felt instead diminutive and abandoned, and as if the world were indifferent to his existence. The feeling frightened the boy, prompting him to call for his father.

His father knelt beside him. "I think he went off to the right there," he said, breathing heavily and pointing with

Robert Boisvert

his chin to a darker section of the woods. The man's red face seemed to glow like a heat lamp. A droplet of mucus hung from the tip of his nose. "I think he's circling round to the pool at the bottom of the East Gorge. If we hurry and take the shortcut down the cliff face, we might be able to be in place by the time he arrives." The man was smiling. "You okay, boy?"

The boy felt cold and wet, and was gripping his rifle as if it were a security blanket. He felt frightened by the idea of descending the cliff face, and was wishing they would return to the campsite and light a fire, despite the earliness of the day. But he didn't object to the plan for fear of disappointing his father, and nodded his head and stood up. "I'm alright," he said, his teeth chattering.

Hoyle halted the gray. The black mood did not lessen as he arrived in the open on the first of the Skulls. Dismounting the horse and taking off its saddle and bridle, and allowing it to roam free to graze on the short grass beneath the last of the trees, he led the bay onto the rocks near the second tier of the plateau where he unloaded his father's rifle and the body, letting it fall to the ground. Removing the tack from the bay, and allowing it too to wander off, its shoes slipping and clicking on the rocks, he hauled the body up onto the top tier of the plateau before retrieving the rifle and taking the pen and paper and envelope from the game bag and sitting on the warm stone.

He'd shot at Travis to convince him of his desperation, and to make sure he followed him. His plan now was to leave a note for his friend, taking full blame for killing Shawn. He would seal the note in the envelope, attach it to the blue tarp, and slip off into the woods. He knew he could survive with the few items he now possessed for as long as it took for him to lose whoever might tail him, and to make his way into Tennessee, or up north along the Appalachian Trail. He remembered that fellow Eric Rudolph who set off the bomb at the Olympics in Atlanta and how long he'd survived in these same mountains before getting caught. Hoyle imagined he'd avoid the same fate by emerging from the woods sooner rather than later, and blending into society by adopting a new identity and surviving by working odd and menial jobs, and by the fact that far fewer authorities would be searching for him.

He stared at the paper, fluttering in the breeze, trying to figure what to write. It had first seemed obvious and simple: "I killed Shawn. He threatened to kill me and my daughter, and I was forced to kill him in self defense." But now he worried about the nuance and shades of meaning of each word, and how they might be interpreted, and whether they would satisfy any questions Travis and other investigators might have. Hadn't Travis already said, "Maybe Christine couldn't take it anymore," meaning he believed Christine was responsible for Shawn's death. What if he still believed that, even after finding the note? Shouldn't the note also explain why he put Christine on a bus and gave her money and placed Shawn's car on the highway, and that he'd been planning on hiding Shawn's body in a crevice in the mountains? Shouldn't he be sure it left no room for doubt about his guilt?

Hoyle felt lost and uncertain and tried calming himself by thinking of Christine and imagining the new life she would lead, bought by his actions. He tried imagining her on the train and being befriended by a college student or a wise and kindly older woman. He then thought about her meeting a good man, and holding a child of her own, and singing to the child, and feeding and raising the child, but soon gave up, each scene seeming more staged and false than the last, like segments of a television show. He felt confused and a growing desperation, fueled by the black mood and now aggravated by the stink of the body blown towards him by the southerly breeze.

He stood and approached the thing, hating it. What confused him most was the greater why beyond the present situation. He understood what had brought him here, and the necessity of it. He didn't question why Christine shot Shawn, or even why Shawn acted the way he did. He knew he was right to send her away, and Diane too, no matter the harm he caused.

But why it all made sense and progressed and added up the way it did left him feeling aggrieved and angry, as if he'd been forced to follow a maze without end and for no reason. His anger grew until he hated everything and everyone so that he wanted to rip open the tarp and smash Shawn's face with the rifle butt, turning it into pulp, and to load the rifle and shoot at everything that moved, including the horses.

Hoyle returned to where he'd left the game bag and tried again to compose the note. He wrote, "I killed Shawn," and thought about everything that might need to be included in it, mentally composing and crossing out one paragraph after another. But he knew already it would do no good, knew by the time he heard the whine of the approaching ATVs that his guilt wouldn't be sealed in other people's minds with just a note, and that there would remain the possibility the authorities would still chase after Christine if he left it attached to the body, and escaped into the woods. He remembered something Shawn had said to him. What had he said? Something about Christine never being safe because Hoyle wasn't willing to cross a line. He knew now his admission of guilt would require an act much more desperate than the note and two errant shots at Travis, and reached into the game bag for a box of ammunition.

Hoyle saw a figure in a brown uniform dart to behind a tree near the end of the logging road, then another in the woods to his left. He began loading the rifle.

"Hoyle!" he heard. He recognized Travis's voice amplified by a bullhorn. "Drop the rifle and come on down! We can talk about this. Hoyle! There's men all around you. There's no way you can get away."

Hoyle knew Travis was lying, knew men would not have been able to work their way around him without breaking into the open and being seen. He lay on the rock in the prone position, scanning the tree line for any sight of Travis. It occurred to him that there was a good chance Travis hadn't told anyone about his suspicions about Christine, and that if he killed him he wouldn't need to worry about his daughter. He knew from the sound of the bullhorn in what direction Travis was hiding, but couldn't yet see him.

Hoyle thought about the shot. He imagined squeezing the trigger and seeing a spray of red and his friend tumble backwards. He thought about what he would then need to do, and about grabbing the game bag and running behind him for the woods. He pictured himself scrambling downhill and trying to keep his balance, then climbing over rocks and fallen trees and up escarpments, feeling winded and knowing the men behind him wouldn't give up. He also thought about Diane and wondered if she'd been right about how he might have felt about her, if given the chance, and whether he'd been wrong to reject her invitation.

He lowered the rifle to rest his wounded arm, which was aching and sending spasms down his side. He felt tired all of a sudden, and wanted to turn on his back and stare at the sky until his eyes hurt from the blue of it, and sleep. Smelling the body again, and inhaling and exhaling deeply, he turned his head towards it, as if to say, "Okay, you win."

"Come on, boy," his father said. "We're almost there."

Hoyle saw his father walking in front of him, heard the crunch of his footsteps in the snow and frozen duff. The boy wanted to stop, wanted to beg his father to light a fire so that he could thaw his toes stinging with pain in his socks and rubber boots. He hurried to keep pace, sucking in mouthfuls of cold air that chilled his lungs and belly and groin, seeming to pucker them as if to draw them inside out.

Robert Boisvert

They were descending the east side of the second Skull, approaching to where the terrain dropped about fifty feet into a rocky gorge that smelled year round like wet and rusty iron. Walking sideways on the steep ground, grabbing hold of saplings to keep from skidding, they moved slowly now, testing each step on the frozen and fallen leaves to be sure they didn't slip on hidden rocks. The boy felt as if his body were morphing into the ground and as if his feet were transforming into and molding to the rock so that he needed to pause at each footfall and break them free to move forward. He didn't care any longer about the buck, knew they were already too late to catch it, and that they should turn around and return to their campsite.

"It will be okay. Just take your time," his father said, as they stepped out of the trees and arrived at the cliff where the sunlight offered no comfort, and seemed to be filtered through gray water. "I'll be right behind you, holding onto your belt."

The boy stared at the first of a number of natural steps in the cliff face that descended to a ledge about fifteen feet from the floor of the gorge. He'd played on the steps the previous summer, been excited by their height, but now felt terrified by the idea of placing any weight onto them, and moved forward only because he felt too ashamed not to. Holding his rifle by its barrel in his left hand, and gripping the cliff face with his right, he moved gingerly, certain the steps were about to give way and plunge him into a never-ending nothingness, despite his father's grip on his trousers.

"Keep your eyes on the next step. Don't look down," his father said. "You're doing fine. Good boy."

The boy felt as if he might burst into tears at any moment by the time they reached the ledge, and shook his head when his father held out his hand.

"Take my hand," the man said. "I'll lower you down."

The boy shook his head.

"Hoyle, take my hand. It will be alright. I promise."

The boy reached for his father, but regretted it even before the man grabbed hold of his arm and pushed him beyond the lip of the ledge. He wanted to scream as he was lowered along the last few feet of the cliff, and kicked his feet looking for purchase, feeling a terror that seemed to bite and swallow him like a monster shark.

"Pull me up, Daddy," he said. "Please, Daddy. Pull me up. I'm going to fall."

His father squeezed his arm so that it hurt. "Stop squirming. You aren't going to fall. Look at me," he said. "Look at me."

The boy looked at his father, surprised that he wasn't angry, the man's eyes seeming as kind and assured as when he bid him goodnight each night.

"Now listen. I'm going to let go of you. There'll be a short drop. You won't be hurt." The man shook his head. "Listen to me," he repeated, louder this time, just as the boy was about to object. "You'll be fine. I promise you. Nothing bad will happen. When you get on the ground, get ready for me to pass you the rifles. Ready?"

The boy was certain he would fall forever.

"Ready?"

Hoyle knew he couldn't kill his friend, no matter how much he hated him, knew there was only one way to save his daughter. He scanned the tree line, guessing at least five deputies were training their weapons on him. Seated now on the top tier of the plateau, the rifle on his lap, he was trying to fathom the concept of ever again opening his eyes. He'd wanted to sleep, craved to close his eyes and shed his consciousness and drift off into forgetfulness. But now he feared even blinking, having been terrified by the idea of never reopening them, or of dreaming. He felt horrified by the blackness. And even more so by the absence of it, and of everything, and the notion of a place that wasn't a place where nothing could no longer be defined. It did not seem possible. It did not seem fair. Was this it? Nothing else? Could this be it? He wanted more. Wanted to keep hoping and trying. Did not want to relinquish what seemed rightfully his and his alone. How could he be expected to give up everything he wasn't and wasn't yet?

He scuttled away from the edge of the plateau, out of sight of the deputies. He thought about Christine and Diane, saw in his mind a flickering series of images of what might and perhaps should have been. Why hadn't he boarded the bus with Christine and vanished then into the crowds? They wouldn't have found them. Or why had he refused Diane's offer to take her and Christine to the beach? It was so stupid to say no. He saw himself gazing at the ocean, his back to the houses painted pink and yellow and blue. He saw himself toeing the wet sand, then swimming in the surf, and diving through the waves, muscling into the broader swells and darker, colder water. He also wondered why he didn't now just stand up and shoot blindly into the woods and wait for the deputies to return fire. So what if it was cowardly, or didn't guarantee certainty. Wasn't the other too much to ask of anyone?

"Are you ready?"

The boy said nothing, despite his terror, and waited for his father to release him. Time seemed to move at a different pace during and after the drop. The drop itself lasted only a second or so, but the sensation of his falling and his reaction to it seemed to last many moments longer, so that he felt as if he were tumbling end-over-end even while standing on solid ground and looking up at his father. The boy glanced around in all directions, as if to be sure nothing were about to leap out at him. Right away, he could smell the water from the pool about fifty yards to his left near the trail that wound around the mountain at a more gentle slope from which they hoped the buck would soon emerge.

"Here," his father said, crouching on the ledge, "take the rifles, and take them over there by that boulder."

The boy turned to look at the boulder about the size of a cow laying in a field girded by two scrub pines. He approached the base of the cliff and reached for the first rifle, feeling ashamed of his earlier fear and what he said and how he acted, and wanted now to seem strong and useful. But he stumbled several times as he reached up on the flinty and slippery ground that sloped at a steep angle at the base and gave way each time he stood on tiptoe, so that he nearly dropped his father's rifle and scratched its stock on the surrounding rocks, causing him further embarrassment. He carried both rifles to the boulder, wishing the day would hurry and end.

He did not see his father swing himself over the ledge and turned only when he heard the man hit the ground, and the sounds of his boots sinking into the flinty soil and of his legs careening backwards, slapping the ground and slipping, trying to regain their balance. He saw his father cartwheel his arms, and spin his body at the last moment, hitting the ground hard on his knees and elbows, and sliding forward. The boy stared at the man, shocked by the sight of his prostrate form and by the sound that had burst from him like that of dog coughing up a bone.

The man rolled over onto the small of his back, holding his hands like a surgeon not wanting to dirty them. His hands were scraped, as was his left cheek. His hat sat askew on his head, and he'd torn both elbows of his jacket. But the boy stared only at the man's left knee that seemed to be streaming blood through a matting of dirt and gravel. Blood already coated the lower portion of the trouser, making it appear as if were shellacked. His father sat up and picked at the dirt and the ragged cloth to peer at the gash.

"Damn it," he muttered. He made to stand, but dropped back down. "Bring me my rifle, boy."

The boy didn't move.

"Come on, boy," his father said, waving a hand, "help me out. Bring me my rifle."

The boy trotted to retrieve the rifle, holding it out to him.

"Closer," the man said.

The boy stepped closer, feeling nauseated by the heat and the odors of sweat and blood emanating from his father. The man used the rifle as a cane to lift himself from the ground and limp to the boulder. Stripping out of his jacket and flannel shirt, then replacing the jacket, he pulled a knife from his pocket before settling to the ground and leaning against the boulder. He used the knife to slice the shirt into long strips. The boy could not stop staring at the gash and the bulbs of white meat surrounding it.

"It's not as bad as it looks," his father said. "I'll be alright." He began cutting away pieces of his ripped trouser leg.

"Should I gather wood for a fire?" the boy asked. He wanted to be helpful, and to be given direction.

The man shook his head. He was peering at the gash and picking out bits of rock and dirt. "No, what you really need to do is keep an eye out for that buck. And keep your voice down. He should be along pretty soon now. Hopefully, he won't smell us."

The boy couldn't figure if his father was joking, and if he was trying to be brave to keep him from worrying. "How are we going to get home?"

"It'll be alright. Nothing's broken. Once I stanch the blood, I should be able to limp pretty good."

"Ma's going to be mad." The boy didn't believe his father, and couldn't stop his mind from leaping from one seeming disaster to another. He saw them hunkering in the dark, cold and hungry and thirsty. He saw himself trying to support his father on the trek down the mountains, and stumbling and failing, and having to fetch his mother, and her worried and angry reaction. He also imagined how forlorn he would feel if she later forbade them from ever again traveling into the woods and hunting together.

His father smiled. "She'll really be mad if she ever finds out I swung you from that ledge. Don't you say nothing, now. Hear? Let me do the talking."

"I think we should go, Dad. I think we should start for home."

His father was now wrapping the strips of shirt around his knee. He winced when he tied the last one in place.

"Don't look at me, boy. I'll be fine. Look out there."

"But I think we should go, Dad. I think we should head home."

"Hoyle, that ain't for you to decide. Quit worrying."

"But it's a long walk. What if you can't make it?"

The man gripped the boy's ankle, squeezing it. "That ain't your job. Understand? We're here now. You deserve this. You've earned it. Now do as I say. Keep an eye out for that buck."

The boy continued gazing at his father.

"Go on," the man said. "Don't look at me. Set your sights over yonder on the pool."

"But how will you get a shot off? How will you aim and set yourself for a shot?"

His father flexed his leg, then shook his head. "Forget about the shot. Forget about me. I'm fine exactly where I am." He lifted and resettled himself using the palms of his hands. "Anyway, it ain't always important to get off a shot. Sometimes just looking is enough. Sometimes that's more important."

The boy turned toward the pool. He did it only because he was asked to do it, and because he didn't want to be scolded, but soon was searching the trail for any sign of movement, feeling a growing twinge of excitement in his belly about the size of what might step forward out of the woods.

"Think about it," he heard his father say. "This might be your only opportunity ever in your life to see one as big and beautiful as this. You don't want to miss it, do you?"

Hoyle heard Travis calling on the bullhorn, telling him he was surrounded. He was writing now, grasping the pen and paper and envelope he'd stuffed into the game bag, and hoping he wasn't wrong. It was a gamble. The act was desperation itself. Yes. And he would cross the line. But he knew he couldn't be certain of any outcome. He wrote fast, trying to make the notes as legible as possible, despite his trembling hand and the thrumming of his heart that seemed about to pop his eardrums. He felt a fool. He felt pathetic and ashamed of his terror and of the fact he couldn't now conjure enough spit to lick and seal the envelope, no matter how hard he tried, and prayed it would not be held against him.

* * * * * * * * * *

Travis heard the shot just as he keyed the bullhorn to call out again to Hoyle. Ducking, and lowering the horn, he instead radioed the six teams of two men spread to his left and right to find out if anyone was hit and in which direction the shot had headed.

No one knew or was hurt.

His partner, a young recruit just graduated from two years of community college, said, "Maybe the crazy fucker is trying to make a break for it. You know? Shoot at us so we'll duck for cover, then sneak off into the woods."

Travis couldn't discount what the kid said, considering Hoyle had backed out of sight only moments ago, but resented how the kid referred to his friend, even if his friend had taken two shots at him earlier at the house. Neither came close, which caused him then to wonder what Hoyle had really been aiming at, knowing Hoyle to be an excellent shot. The shots surprised him, that's for sure. As did Hoyle's escape into the woods. All told, he couldn't figure what the man was attempting to accomplish, except to protect his daughter.

"You stay here," he said to the kid. He then glanced at the black assault rifle the kid was hugging like a teddy bear, and added, "Don't shoot. Hear me? I don't want to get caught in the middle of a damned battle. Just shout out if you see anything."

After radioing his other men and telling them the same, then saying a silent prayer, he ran forward to a rock about knee high to his right, waited a few moments, then ran to a slightly larger rock to his left. Feeling frightened, and angry because he was placed in a situation which caused him to feel frightened, he took off his hat and peered beyond the top of the rock, scanning for any movement. He could see a good portion of the plateau from where he was. He saw a saddle and bridle at the base of it and, above them and to the left, something wrapped in blue tarp he guessed to be Shawn. Beyond that and to the right, and not moving, he saw the soles of two work boots.

"Hoyle!" Travis shouted. "Hoyle, don't shoot! It's me! I just want to talk!"

Waiting a few moments, and after radioing his men and telling them what he planned, he picked up a palm sized rock and threw it at the boots. He waited a few more moments before throwing another, but knew already what had happened. Jogging half crouched toward the plateau, though this time with less caution, and getting his first whiff of the stink of whatever was wrapped in the tarp, he saw the blood spread on the stone beyond the boots.

Travis radioed his men to break cover and come forward.

Stepping onto the plateau and past the tarp, and noting the paper tucked beneath the twine holding it closed, Travis shook his head as he approached Hoyle's body, feeling guilty for a reason he couldn't pinpoint. Travis knelt beside the body, taking in the envelope tucked in the man's waistband, the rifle still pointed at the head, the scorch marks beneath his chin, and the much larger exit wound through the top of the head. Travis stared at the man's face, surprised to see it wasn't as agonized as he would have expected.

"Jesus," he heard the kid behind him say. "The top of his head is like a foot away."

Travis turned to see him and the other men gathered around the body and gazing at it as if they were sorry they hadn't brought their cameras.

The kid was now holding the note that had been tucked into the tarp. "'I killed Shawn,'" he read. "'I'm sorry. It was no one's fault but my own.' Well, no shit Sherlock." The kid was bent at the waist and directing the remark at Hoyle's body as if expecting it to hear him and feel regret for what seemed the stupidity of the last line of the note.

Travis pointed to another deputy. "Jimmy, call the sheriff and let him know what happened. Then call the coroner and head on down to the road to wait for him."

"Hey, there's another one here," the kid said, crouching across from Travis and taking the envelope from Hoyle's waistband. "'To Christine,'" he read.

Travis took the envelope from the kid before he could open it. He could discern the blue ink on the paper inside the envelope, the color looking vibrant in the sun.

"Who's Christine?" the kid asked.

Travis looked at the tarp, hating all the vileness and meanness that combined to create what used to be the person contained within it. He thought about Christine, and what he might have done differently, if he'd have been in Hoyle's shoes. Or if Shawn or someone just as mean had set his sights on one of his boys. He knew the answer wasn't easy, not nearly as easy as most people would have guessed, and was reminded of the last time he'd hit one of his sons for doing something the boy knew he shouldn't be doing, and the look the boy gave him, and the years it took for him to rebuild their relationship. He also remembered the temptation to hit him again on several occasions, knowing the boy deserved it. He looked again at Hoyle, wishing he'd done more to help his friend, despite not knowing how he might have helped.

Travis fingered the letter, turning now to look out over the valley.

He shook his head. "I don't know. Probably no one we need worry about."